Only Human

KATE THOMPSON

RED FOX

ONLY HUMAN
A RED FOX BOOK 0 009943224 2

First published in Great Britain by The Bodley Head
an imprint of Random House Children's Books

Bodley Head edition published 2001
Red Fox edition published 2002

3 5 7 9 10 8 6 4 2

Copyright © Kate Thompson, 2001

Papers used by Random House Children's Books are natural,
recyclable products made from wood grown in sustainable forests.
The manufacturing processes conform to the environmental
regulations of the country of origin.

Red Fox Books are published by Random House Children's Books,
61–63 Uxbridge Road, London W5 5SA,
a division of The Random House Group Ltd,
in Australia by Random House Australia (Pty) Ltd,
20 Alfred Street, Milsons Point, Sydney, NSW 2061, Australia,
in New Zealand by Random House New Zealand Ltd,
18 Poland Road, Glenfield, Auckland 10, New Zealand,
and in South Africa by Random House (Pty) Ltd,
Endulini, 5A Jubilee Road, Parktown 2193, South Africa

THE RANDOM HOUSE GROUP Limited Reg. No. 954009
www.kidsatrandomhouse.co.uk

A CIP catalogue record for this book is available from the British Library.

Printed in Great Britain by Clays Ltd, St Ives plc

For Lucy

PART ONE

1

We ate no meat of any kind in Fourth World, but our dairy and our gardens provided for most of our needs. The rest, the best, came from the Atlantic.

Danny was our fisherman. He went out at night when there was no danger that anyone would see what happened when he entered the water. On land he was awkward; a lumbering hulk of a teenager who somehow wasn't put together quite right, all out of step with himself and everyone else. But at sea, the dolphin genes that had been given to him before his birth came into their own. In the cold waters of the Atlantic, Danny was in his element.

Sometimes he stayed there for hours, swimming far out into the deepest, darkest currents where the herring ran, and the cod and wild salmon. He could have lived at sea, he told us. But he always came back, lugging his catch along the silent glen in the dark, creeping through the sleeping house to his bed before the birds began to sing.

Once I walked down the path with him, just for company's sake. It was a clear, still night and the sea was quiet, examining the stars that lay reflected on its dark surface like new ideas. We sat on the shore together, examining them too, until Danny said,

'There's something out there that sings.'

'Sings?' I said. 'Is it the whales, Danny?'

He shook his head. 'Whales sing, and dolphins do, too. But this is different. This is something . . .'

He looked into my face and then past it, and I waited for the word he was searching for. But he didn't find it.

'Something else,' was all he said.

2

It was early summer, and I was in the garden sweating over my hoe when Loki came hurtling down the hillside towards me.

'Thither-up!' she panted. 'Crampy gurgle-tube!'

I put aside the hoe and reached out a hand to her, but she was twisting around my legs like a small, dark tornado.

'Loki, stop,' I said, managing to grab hold of an ear. 'What's happening?'

She yelped and crouched at my feet.

'Whisker-hunt,' she said.

'Whose whiskers?' I asked. 'What have you done?'

She tried to mime it, racing up and down, leaping and pouncing, then gazing intently at the fallen hoe and wagging her tail. But the little drama was meaningless to me. I sighed and shook my head.

'I don't understand, Loki.'

She looked sad and perplexed, and my heart ached for her. There had been an unusual connection between us since we had first met, a few days after she was born. We had both known

5

it. She was my dog, I was her boy. We had rapidly become inseparable. She was the brightest of the litter from the very start, streets ahead of her brothers and sisters in learning how to talk and to count and to work things out for herself. Until the accident, that was.

It still sent a shock through my veins when I remembered it. Sandy and I had been out in the woods all day, working one at each end of the bush saw. We had put up a mighty heap of firewood and I was exhausted. Sandy's frog muscle seemed to give her enormous stamina as well as strength, and working with her was like trying to keep pace with a machine. So I was relieved when Tony arrived with his little cart to bring home the logs.

He stood patiently in the shafts while we loaded up. Sandy picked and tossed with her usual vigour, but my arms were like jelly after the day's work, and I was completely butter-fingered. Loki realised I was in trouble and started retrieving the logs I dropped, even though she could barely get her little jaws around them. She was about three months old at the time.

I dropped one too many. The last one rolled under Tony's feet, and he decided to help, too, by pawing it back out to me. But Loki went for it at the same time, and Tony's hoof connected with her skull instead of the log.

He was mortified, poor thing. He thought he had killed her. So did I. She hadn't even yelped.

She just sprawled where she had fetched up, quivering slightly. Her tongue was lolling and her eyes were open, but there was no sign of intelligence in them. I knelt beside her, frantic with concern. She was breathing, and her heart was beating. There was some chance, at least.

I forgot my exhaustion and ran home with her to Maggie. She laid Loki out on the kitchen table and examined her minutely. There was a soft swelling on the side of her head, and Maggie said that the bone had caved in underneath it. She made the pup comfortable in a box above the range, but confessed that she didn't hold out much hope for her.

I stayed up after the others had gone to bed, and draped Loki across my knees on the kitchen floor. I knew that she could hear me, even if she couldn't answer, and I talked to her non-stop about all the things we had done together and all the things we would still do, if only she would come back from whatever between-worlds place it was that she had gone to.

And she did come back. The next morning she was trying to lift her head, and her feet were twitching as though she were dreaming, or trying to run back to us from her waiting death. Over the next few days she managed to sit up, and I fed her with milk and soft flakes of fish. But she could neither speak nor understand what was said to her.

I couldn't be a full-time nurse to her. I was needed outside in the gardens. It was Tina who had the idea of leaving the radio on to keep her company, and Maggie who extended the idea and suggested tapes instead, to re-establish Loki's vocabulary. Maggie loved to listen while she was working, and had a small library of books on tape down in the lab. So, for the next few weeks, Loki lived in the sitting room, and while the rest of us were out at work, she kept company with Shakespeare and Tolstoy, Barrett Browning and the Brontes, Melville and Manley Hopkins.

It worked.

Well, almost.

'Try again, Loki,' I said, laying a hand on her head.

'Wurra-wurra-wurra,' she barked, chasing some imaginary creature around in small circles.

'Relax, Loki. Calm down.'

She parked herself tight against my legs and gazed up into my eyes.

'Hackle-scrap,' she said. 'Timorous tremblepuss.'

'Puss?' I asked.

She resorted to mimicry. The plaintive little sound was far easier to understand than all her previous efforts.

'Miaow?'

3

Loki led the way back up the hill-side and I followed her. I didn't like to admit it but she was becoming a bit of a liability. The blow to her head had affected more than her ability to form sentences. It seemed to have knocked a lot of the sense out of her as well.

All the animals of Fourth World learned to follow certain basic codes of behaviour. You didn't steal things. You didn't go charging all over the vegetable gardens, but kept to the paths. You didn't get into fights with other animals; not serious ones, anyway. Even Sparky, and Obi and Kanobi, who were Loki's relations and weren't talking dogs, understood these things. But Loki didn't.

Nor did she understand about meal-times or bed-times, or about the difference between night and day. All the animals had their own bowls and their own beds, but Loki was notorious for taking the wrong ones and created constant friction among the animals. The humans, too. She would steal food from the table at every opportunity, and tear around the house in the middle of the night, shouting

'Roustabout!' or 'Moonstalking!' or 'Man-the-barricades!'

We had tried putting her outside at night, but that was worse. Every sound she heard became a threat to Fourth World, and she ran around and barked incessantly, annoying everyone and making it impossible for Obi and Kanobi and Oggy and Itchy to get on with the real work of listening out for threatening sounds.

And although nobody ever blamed me, I felt responsible all the same. Loki was my dog. More and more, as time went on, she was becoming my problem.

'Hi, Christie!'

I turned and saw Sandy bounding towards me across the steep fields. In three or four more powerful jumps she was at my side.

'Where are you going?'

I nodded towards Loki, ahead of me on the hill-side. 'She seems to have found more trouble.'

'What's new?' said Sandy and set off again, up the hill ahead of me.

I followed, annoyed by my own pathetic, human pace. I had grown fond of Sandy over the months that I had been at Fourth World, but it didn't mean she didn't get on my nerves. I was well aware of how much stronger and faster she was than me, but I couldn't see why she had to keep on rubbing it in. At least, at times like this one I couldn't. In the quiet of my own thoughts I understood it very well.

At the top of the hill she stopped and called back to me.

'Come on, slow-coach!'

'All right, all right,' I called back. 'I'm only human, you know!'

She was well ahead of me again by the time I reached the heather-clad slopes above the meadows. Loki was with her, and came haring back to lick my hand and hurry me along.

'King's high-by-way,' she said. 'Squeezle-tib liberation crusade.'

'OK, Loki. I'm coming. I'm coming.'

'Suffocat!' she said. 'Urgent-emergency!'

Then she was gone again, jinking along the twisting path like a hunted hare, heading for the dam. I followed as quickly as I could, astonished, as usual, by her boundless energy.

I didn't know where she got it from and sometimes, I had to admit, it was worrying. I couldn't count the number of times I had lectured her on the importance of staying close to the house and of never, never talking in front of anyone who wasn't one of us; part of the Fourth World family. She understood, as she understood most things that were said to her, but there was no way of knowing whether she remembered. I kept my concerns to myself, but I was sure the disastrous possibilities must have occurred to the others as well.

It was crucial to our existence here at Fourth

11

World that no one should discover what Maggie and her partner, Bernard, had produced. If the outside world found out about the missing link, the gene that enabled animals to speak and reason as humans did, there was no telling what might happen. Only one thing was certain. Our peaceful, self-sufficient life here would come to an abrupt end.

4

'Miaow!' said Loki, standing above a discarded length of pipe left over from the installation of the hydro-electric scheme. Sandy was peering into one end. 'Stupid dog,' she said.

I was still out of breath and more irritated than ever. 'She's not stupid. She's just . . .'

'Just what?' Sandy stood up and walked to where the other end of the pipe disappeared into a well-established tangle of undergrowth. I knelt down where she had been and looked into the dark opening.

'Oedipus?'

'Miaow.'

This time the sound really was made by a cat. It was muted, and came from at least half-way along the pipe.

'Scuffle-scratch! Spittle-hiss!' said Loki, miming the encounter which, presumably, had resulted in Oedipus taking refuge in the pipe.

'You shouldn't chase him, Loki. I keep telling you that.'

'Scoundrel-tib,' said Loki. 'Harum-scarum!' She made a mock dive at the end of the pipe.

'No, Loki. No!'

She sighed and threw herself down on to the coarse grass.

'Extractapuss?' she said.

There was nothing to be seen inside the pipe. The other end had been completely closed over by the tangled grass and heather.

'Come out, Oedipus,' I called.

'Stuck!' he yowled, his voice distorted by the long hollow of the pipe. 'Can't turn round.'

'Then reverse out.'

'Reverse?'

'Yes. Reverse. Go backwards.'

'I know what "reverse" means, Christie.'

'Then why don't you?'

Sandy gave the pipe a savage kick. 'Just come out, you thick-head!'

There was a long silence.

'Oedipus?' I said.

'What?' he spat.

'Come on. Back out, will you?'

'I will not,' said Oedipus. 'I have my dignity to consider.'

Dignity. I was kneeling in the mud, talking into the end of an old pipe, and he was concerned about dignity.

'I don't think there's anything particularly dignified about starving to death. Do you?'

'Sarcophopuss,' said Loki.

'Get rid of her!' Oedipus mewled. 'Get rid of that mad dog!'

'If I do, will you come out?'

There was another long pause, and then a

14

small voice came back. 'I might. But don't kick the pipe again, OK?'

'Go away, Loki,' I said. 'Go home.'

She pricked her ears and looked at me, tilting her head to one side and then the other.

'You heard me. Go back to the house.'

Her ears flattened, and with a dejected expression she began to slink back down the path. There was a scrabbling sound from inside the pipe as Oedipus began his humiliating return to the daylight world. I could judge his position by the sound of his claws and, despite his objections, he was making rapid progress.

'All right, puss?' I said.

'Don't look.'

I turned away and caught Sandy's eye. We were both grinning, trying our hardest not to laugh. Loki was barely twenty yards away, dawdling along at a snail's pace that must have taken great concentration for her to maintain. By the sound of things, Oedipus was almost at the mouth of the pipe when Loki's head snapped up and she began a fast and furious barking.

The cat shot back down to the end of the pipe. I stood up, ready to reprimand Loki, convinced that she was up to her old mischief again. But as soon as I was on my feet I could see what it was that she was barking at. Along the glen, two figures were approaching Fourth World.

5

It was very unusual for us to get visitors. Soon
after Danny and Tina and I arrived at Fourth
World, three men had attempted a night raid on
the greenhouses, but since then we had
encountered no intruders. From time to time,
someone would walk up from Bettyhill with
something to barter for some of our vegetables.
Usually it was fish, and usually Maggie was
happy to trade. We had vegetables coming out
of our ears at that time of year, and although
we had plenty of fish as well, it suited us not to
divulge that in case anyone should start wondering where we got it from. Maggie said that
a few vegetables was a small price to pay for
being on good terms with the neighbours. And
although she didn't encourage people to come,
she never turned anyone away, either.

'Shh, Loki,' I said, standing beside her,
stroking her dented skull. Between her frantic
barks, she spat out bits of disjointed vocabulary.

'Treachery! To horse! To horse! Marauder-
men!'

'I don't think so,' I said.

Sandy was crouching beside her with a look of intense concentration on her face.

'Is it them?' she said.

'Who?'

I could see now that it was a man and a boy who were approaching. I couldn't be sure, but I didn't think I had seen them before. Their hands were empty and they both had large rucksacks on their backs which was, I thought, an odd way to carry fish. And there was something else that was odd. Several birds were fluttering above their heads, hopping from branch to branch, keeping pace with them. A small red shape that I suspected was a fox was occasionally visible through the trees, and behind it was a black-and-white dog. It might have been Oggy, the sheepdog who had come to Ireland to fetch Danny home, and it might have been his sister, Itchy. But I had a feeling that it was neither of them. They had, I had heard, another sister, Titch, but I had never seen her. I knew where she had gone, though. And I knew who had gone with her.

Loki was still barking savagely, and I could barely hear Sandy's voice above her racket.

'It is! It's them!'

A surge of excitement charged my bones.

'Shut up, Loki! They aren't strangers!'

Sandy was already gone, leaping down the steep hill-side. Loki tore after her, barking wildly.

I glanced back towards the dam. Oedipus's

tail emerged from the pipe, followed by the rest of him. He scowled disdainfully at us, then shook his paws one by one and began to wash them.

'Come on, puss,' I called. 'No time for that, now. Bernard and Colin are home.'

PART TWO

1

I ran as hard as I could, but within a few moments the others, even Oedipus, were out of sight in the valley below. At the bottom of the hill I raced through the orchard and on to the path that led to the house. Then I stopped and somehow managed to find the breath to whistle for Loki.

I was brimming with excitement. It was going to be a great homecoming. Three of us had made the arduous journey from Ireland to Fourth World: Danny, my step-brother, Tina, the homeless girl who had befriended Oggy in Dublin, and I. Danny was Colin's half-brother, but none of us had met Bernard and Colin. They had set out on a research expedition before we arrived and had been away ever since. They belonged to Fourth World and, as far as I was concerned, they were part of my new family.

I knew that but Loki didn't. I didn't really expect her to come to my call, so when she did, I praised her.

'Stay with me now, Loki. You hear?'

'Ring-alarum!' she growled, trying to swallow her barks. 'Hedge-knights!'

'They're family, Loki. Sandy's brother and her father.'

'Kithkin,' she said, but she had inherited, from her Doberman parents, a tendency to be suspicious. As we raced along the narrow path towards the glen, she was still grumbling threateningly and her hackles were stiff.

I was considering getting hold of her collar when I rounded a bend and everyone came into view. Maggie and Danny were standing with the newcomers and Tina was hanging back, watching. I couldn't see Sandy anywhere, but before I had time to wonder where she was, Loki spotted the fox. She stopped for one astonished moment and her hackles bristled. Then, with an explosive shout that sounded something like 'Public-enemy!' she hurled herself straight at it. The fox decided against negotiation, whipped round, and fled.

'Loki!' I yelled. 'Loki!'

She might as well have been deaf. As I caught up with the others she disappeared into the scrub down beside the river.

'I'm sorry,' I said, singling out the man I took to be Bernard. 'She's just a bit . . .I mean, she had an accident . . .'

'Don't worry,' said Bernard.

'She's unruly, but she's not bad,' I babbled. 'I mean . . .Even if she caught him, I don't think . . .'

I shut my mouth, aware that Bernard wasn't listening. He was gazing intently at Maggie and she was gazing back. Abruptly they both stepped forward and into each other's arms. I felt the colour rise into my cheeks and looked away, careful not to meet anyone's eye. But I couldn't help sneaking another look. I was amazed at how well they fitted together. On the rare occasions when I had tried to hug someone, some bit or the other always got in the way; a nose or an elbow or a hat or a pair of spectacles. Not so with Maggie and Bernard. They fitted and they stayed fitted. Maybe that was what it meant when two people were said to be made for each other?

Eventually they broke apart and Maggie moved on to hug Colin. I held out a hand to Bernard and began to introduce myself, but his attention was somewhere behind me.

I turned. Sandy had emerged from the shadows and was gazing at her father with a mixture of pleasure and anxiety. I moved aside, expecting him to welcome her, but his eyes slid away from her and back to me. Maggie stepped in and introduced me, and Bernard's strong, hot hand engulfed my cold, bony one. He had a black, bushy beard and clear, brown eyes which shone with warmth and acceptance. I could have basked forever in his attention, but he turned it to Danny as Maggie brought him forward. Disappointed, I dropped back and scanned the valley, hoping for a glimpse of Loki and her prey. I didn't see them, but I did see Sandy, standing dejectedly on the edge of the family circle.

'Come on,' I called to her. 'Come and say hello!'

She didn't move. Eventually, Bernard approached her, but she didn't get the hug from him that her mother had. Instead he took her long, skinny hand, gave it a brief squeeze, and said, 'All right, Sandy?'

On the way back to the house I fell in beside Colin, hoping to see some sign of his genetic make-up. I knew that he, like Sandy and Danny, had been an experiment, and that genes from some other species had been introduced into his cells before his birth. But, unlike Sandy and Danny, he showed no evidence of anything unusual in his appearance.

'I'm Christie,' I said.

'Colin.' He extended a hand, as cold and limp as a dead reptile. Now that I was closer I could see something a bit strange. His skin had the faintest tinge of orange, and a strange, silvery sheen in certain lights. It was barely noticeable, and might easily have resulted from exposure to the sun. I would probably have dismissed it entirely if he hadn't drawn my attention back to it.

'I'm part fish,' he said. 'Salmon. I was supposed to have gills, but I didn't work.'

'Oh,' I said.

24

'Got a funny colour instead. You noticed it.'

'Barely.'

'What about you?'

'Me?'

'Yeah. What are you supposed to be?'

'Nothing,' I said. For the second time that day I found myself feeling inferior. 'I'm not supposed to be anything.'

'Oh.' He sounded disappointed.

'Me and Tina,' I said, drawing her into the conversation. 'We're outsiders, you might say.'

'Yeah,' said Tina, shaking hands with Colin. 'We're the new slave labour. Mere mortals.'

. We walked in silence for a while and I realised that Colin was dragging his feet. I wondered how long they had been on the road.

'Can I carry your rucksack?'

'I can manage.' But a few steps further on he stopped to readjust it, and made no objection when I took it from him. It was a bit awkward trying to put it on without disturbing Oedipus, who had draped himself around my shoulders like a living stole.

'Did you find it, then?' said Tina to Colin.

'Find what?'

'What you set out to find. Where the missing link came from.'

Colin shook his head and my spirits took a dive.

'We found something, though. Maybe. A clue.'

'Go on,' said Tina.

'It's better if you wait,' said Colin. 'It's better if you see it for yourselves.'

'What is it?' I asked, my spirits reviving. 'A fossil? A skull or something?'

Colin shook his head. The house was coming into view, and from around the corner of it, Loki and the little fox came trotting up to meet us, the very best of friends.

2

When we had all gathered back at the house, Colin went straight to bed, too exhausted even to eat. The rest of us went into the kitchen, which was now so full of dogs that we had to wade through them to get to the table. Sandy hovered, still waiting for some sign of affection from her father, but as far as I could tell, he ignored her.

As we ate, Bernard told us that they had been at sea for thirteen weeks.

'We hit some dreadful weather,' he said. 'She'll need a bit of work before we set sail again.'

'Who's she?' I said. 'Set sail for where?'

' "She" is *The Privateer*,' said Bernard, and a strange, soft look came into his eyes, a bit like the one that Maggie had when she talked about him. 'She's a twenty-foot, gaff-rigged ketch, refitted from stem to stern. A real beauty.'

'What about where?' I asked.

'That,' said Bernard, 'is for everyone here to decide.'

I noticed that Maggie looked long and hard at him, but he didn't meet her eye and, a bit dejectedly, she returned her attention to her plate.

Loki and I went back to the weeds and the hoe. While I worked, she cavorted around the garden, terrorizing spiders and tossing pebbles for herself. Three times I reminded her to stay out of the vegetable beds. Three times she obliged me, and three times, within five minutes, she forgot.

The third time I dropped the hoe and angrily called her over. She sat at my feet, looking sheepish.

'Why can't you get it into your thick skull?' I snapped. 'Stay away from the vegetables! Get it?'

She wagged her tail and gave a weird, fangy grin and squashed up closer to my legs.

'And while we're at it,' I went on, 'how many times have I told you not to go chasing everything that moves, eh?'

'Nine-seven-nine-threety-twent,' she gabbled.

'So why did you go after that fox?'

At the word 'fox', her ears shot up and she leapt to attention, scanning the surroundings.

'I mean Roxy,' I went on. 'Why did you chase him?'

'Chick-snatch,' she snarled, savagely. 'Rrr . . .rr . . .robber-baron!'

'No, Loki,' I said. 'No, no, no. You're supposed to be civilised, don't you understand that? You're supposed to be able to think.'

Loki put her head to one side and gazed at me earnestly. For a moment, I thought she was really considering what I had said and trying to comply. Then she spotted Hushy floating in on the breeze and shot off across the garden, leaving a scatter of lettuce seedlings in her wake.

I shook my head in despair and bent to retrieve the hoe. 'What am I going to do with you?' I said.

3

In all my life I can hardly remember a day that took so long to pass. The lab, and the work that went on in it, was what tied me most strongly to Fourth World. Since Maggie had first explained to me about the missing link I had been intrigued by the subject. Sometimes I was allowed to go with her to the lab, and I had helped her to introduce the miraculous gene into a thrush's egg. I had been there when Hushy had hatched out, and had watched over him and fed him with worms and insects until he was old enough to go up and take his place among the other creatures of Fourth World. Now he was independent and lived in the woods with the other birds, but I sometimes brought tit-bits to him to make sure that he didn't forget me, and he often accompanied me around the farm, chatting in his repetitive, musical way.

For me, that day was as exciting and frustrating as Christmas Eve, waiting to see what it was that Bernard and Colin had unearthed. I finished the work as fast as I could and went back to the house, but it wasn't an entirely comfortable place. The return of Bernard and

Colin had brought a new tension into it, and everyone was out of sorts. Sandy made herself scarce, and Maggie was still flat, somehow; not quite her usual, spirited self. I tried to winkle her problems out of her, but she wasn't going to be drawn, and we each kept to our own separate thoughts as we prepared the evening meal.

Bernard arrived in to dinner with a pink folder under his arm. He laid it on the table beside his place and, when Maggie and Tina reached for it, dropped a huge, hairy hand on top of it.

'Later,' he said. 'When we're all sitting comfortably.'

I don't think any of us had ever eaten so fast. Even Danny, whose appetite was insatiable, declined a second helping in the interests of haste, and we all agreed to postpone the rhubarb crumble until after the travel tales.

We gathered in the sitting room, crowding around Bernard and Colin on the rug in front of the empty hearth. Sandy was the last to arrive and she stationed herself, purposefully I felt, near the window; at the outside the circle.

As soon as she was settled, Bernard began to speak.

'We sailed from Bettyhill on the twelfth of June and headed out around the coast of Ireland. The weather was fair, the barometer was rising, and we . . .'

31

Maggie interrupted him in an exasperated tone. 'No, Bernard, no. You can't do this to us. Save the sea shanties for another night, will you? Cut to the chase!'

Bernard looked mildly offended, but shrugged it off.

'OK, OK, I'll make it short. We moored off the coast of Africa and took what we could carry ashore. That was when Albert came back to tell you we had arrived.'

'When he came looking for us,' said Tina.

Maggie nodded. Colin said, 'It was horrible inland.'

Bernard laughed, showing his white teeth, which were all crooked. 'Poor old Col. He couldn't handle the heat, could you?'

Colin shook his head. 'We had to travel by night. Good thing we had Roxy and Titch.'

'They were brilliant,' said Bernard. 'Roxy could smell a lion or a snake at a hundred yards. And Titch, well, she's tougher than she looks.'

'She's got the scars to prove it,' said Colin. 'We nearly lost her once.'

'And the birds kept watch during the day,' said Bernard. 'We were sorted, really. Eyes and ears everywhere.'

He was about to go on when a huge commotion started up in the kitchen. There were clatters and crashes, yelps and yips and yowls and yells. We leapt to our feet like a football crowd beginning a Mexican wave. Then the others stepped back and let me go first. It was,

I felt, a dubious honour, but one I undoubtedly deserved.

Because if there was trouble among the animals, it was bound to be caused by Loki.

4

'We have far too many dogs,' said Maggie, following me into the kitchen.

'Just one too many,' snarled Oggy, without taking his eyes from Loki.

She was hemmed into a corner, surrounded by the rest of the bristling pack. On top of the kitchen cabinet, Oedipus and his sister, Electra, were crouching, glaring down at the sea of dogs below. On the floor, among the forest of legs, were a broken casserole dish and a dented pot, dislodged by the cats during their desperate ascent.

'What happened?' I asked.

A clamour of voices responded. I couldn't hear a word that any of them said.

Maggie was right. There were too many dogs. There were three sheepdogs, three non-talking Dobermans and four talking ones; Loki and her siblings. That was ten. Eleven, if you counted Roxy.

'One at a time!' I shouted, above the din. 'Why don't you tell us, Oggy?'

'The cats came in,' he said. 'Roxy went over to introduce himself.'

'Sly-mutt,' growled Loki from her corner. 'Cranium-cruncher.'

'He was very civil,' said Oggy. 'But Loki just flew at him. The cats were terrified.'

'Cautious,' said Oedipus from the heavens. 'Merely taking precautions.'

'But why should you want to protect the cats?' I said to Loki. 'You were chasing Oedipus earlier.'

'Puss-kith,' said Loki. 'Puss-kin.'

Roxy was looking up at me. Butter wouldn't melt in his mouth. On a dark night I wouldn't have trusted him as far as I could throw him, but there was no way he was going to misbehave in an enclosed space surrounded by ten large dogs.

'You've got it wrong again, Loki,' I said.

'Never mind,' said Maggie, gathering up casserole shards. 'They'd better all go out, anyway. Why don't you feed them while I clear up this mess?'

I found two extra bowls in the scullery where the freezers and bottled foods were kept. Then I divvied up the fish and porridge gloop that Maggie boiled for them every morning. The dogs were mad for it but I couldn't understand why. It smelled terrible, and I hated the fact that it was always my job to hand it out.

It had to be, though. No one else would tolerate the inevitable fights that Loki started. She just couldn't learn to eat from the bowl she had been given. Instead, she followed me around, trying to snatch a bit from every bowl as I handed them out, and getting snapped at by everyone. Quite often her own bowl would be empty by the time she got back to it; someone else's reprisal for her greed. Sometimes I let her go hungry, hoping it might teach her something. But it never did.

So this time, I stood guard over her until she had finished. She was mad and she was bad and she was never going to get any better. But in spite of all that, I loved her more with every day that passed.

5

I brought Loki back into the sitting room with me when I rejoined the others.

'No dogs,' said Maggie, but she knew as well as I did that it was the best way to keep Loki out of trouble.

Bernard had been carrying on with the story in my absence.

'You haven't missed much,' he said. 'We made it to the Olduvai Gorge, which is where the oldest human remains have been found.'

'How old?' I asked.

'Anything up to three million years. All kinds of stuff turned up there. Prehistoric man and his forerunners. Ape-men. It appears they over-lapped for a while.'

I settled myself on the floor and Loki sprawled across my lap.

'How long did we spend there, Colin?' Bernard went on.

'Forever,' said Colin. 'The furnaces of hell.'

'It wasn't that hot,' said Bernard. 'I think we were there for about two months altogether. Digging.'

'You were digging,' said Colin. 'I was wilting.'

'And what did you find?' said Tina.

'Not a lot,' said Bernard. 'Bits and pieces. Nothing earth-shattering. The truth is that we really weren't getting anywhere, until we met Malcolm Wainwright. He's an old digger, a fossil himself, practically. He told us about the City of the Apes.'

'Isn't that a film?' I said.

'That's Planet of the Apes, dork,' said Tina.

'Oh, right.'

'The City of the Apes is a kind of legend among some of the tribal peoples in Southern Tanzania,' said Bernard. 'Malcolm had heard that bits of it were still visible in the jungle, and I was intrigued. Ancient cities are rare enough in Africa. I thought it might give us some clues.'

'So off we went again,' said Colin. He seemed to be melting just at the memory of the heat. I liked heat, myself. I wished that I could have been there, adventuring across Africa.

'So, another long trek,' said Bernard. 'More night-time travels. I was worried about how we'd find the city, but when we got into the area the local people were wonderful. Two young men volunteered to guide us there and refused to take any payment at all.'

'Mind you,' said Colin. 'We thought at first that they'd played a practical joke on us.'

'Yes,' said Bernard. 'There wasn't much to be seen, was there?'

'Not a whole lot.'

'Just a few overgrown walls. But we persevered, and after a few days of stumbling around in the undergrowth we finally found it.'

'What?' said three or four different voices, and Loki jumped up and stared around avidly. I don't know what she expected to see.

'It was a cave,' said Colin. 'Or at least not exactly a cave. More like a big, deep overhang of rock. Very sheltered.'

'Used by animals, according to Roxy and Titch. But the walls . . .' Bernard's attention went backwards and inwards, leaving the rest of us stranded.

'Oh, come on,' said Maggie. 'Show us, will you?'

Bernard reached, at last, for the pink folder. We all shuffled closer, forming a tight, eager circle.

6

Bernard opened the folder and took out the first of the black and white photographs. We all craned over, jostling for position, blocking our own light. There wasn't a lot to be seen; just a towering rock covered with lichens and dangling vines.

'Great,' said Tina. 'What are we supposed to be looking at?'

'That's the crag,' said Colin. 'What it looks like when you go up to it.'

Bernard took out the next photo. This one showed the space beneath the overhang. There seemed to be nothing inside it except for shadows. The third photo had us all leaning in again, and Maggie pulled up a table-lamp so we could see. What they had discovered was some kind of carving; a picture engraved upon the solid rock wall.

Loki poked her head beneath my armpit and studied the picture with me. The heat of the huddle was making her pant, and her long pink tongue lolled out above the black and white scene on the floor.

It showed a tall mountain with a wavy line running across it about half way up.

'See the figures?' said Bernard.

There were three of them in the picture; two large and another, slightly smaller one, in between. The lowest of them was clearly human, with long hair which streamed out behind it as though a strong wind was blowing. It held a spear in its hand. The figure at the top was ape-like. It crouched on the high ground, above the wavy line, and was covered all over with long hair. The third one, in the middle, had a big, apparently bald head, and was standing in a deep saucer which balanced on the undulating line.

Bernard's voice was tense, as though he was in the grip of some sort of anxiety. 'What do you make of them?'

We all looked harder, trying to come up with an answer for him, and as we did so, a drip fell from the end of Loki's tongue and splashed on to the print. Maggie took out a handkerchief and dabbed at it.

'Water,' said Loki. 'Swimmery-man.'

'Well done, slobberchops,' I said. 'Now back off, will you?'

Bernard let us look for a while longer, then produced another print. This one was a close-up of the middle figure, and showed him much more clearly. His arms were held straight out on either side, and between his hands, reaching high above his head, was a perfect arch. I wasn't

41

so sure now whether he was bald. Around the upper part of his head there was a second layer, as if his head was sticking into a bubble.

'He's beautiful,' said Danny. 'He's holding a rainbow.'

I noticed that there was some kind of a squiggle on his chest. 'What's that?'

Bernard smiled. 'You put your finger on it, Christie,' he said. 'What's that indeed?'

He produced another photo, this one taken from even closer to the rock. It showed the bald man's outstretched arms and, very clearly, the wiggly pattern on his chest. It reminded me of something, but I couldn't remember what.

Maggie gasped. 'I don't believe it.'

'Nor did I,' said Bernard.

'What?' said Tina. 'What is it?'

'It's a double helix,' said Maggie. 'The structure of DNA.'

'What's DNA?' said Danny.

'It's the stuff we're all made of,' said Bernard. 'The building blocks of genes.'

I peered closer. I could see the similarity, but I wasn't as convinced as the others appeared to be. The two squiggles could just as easily have been random; or a failed attempt to draw two parallel, snaking lines.

'Do you think it's a hoax?' said Maggie.

Bernard shook his head. 'It's very old. There was more at the bottom at one time, but it's mostly been worn away by animals rubbing against the rock.'

'Any idea what was there?'

'Not much. Fishes or whales or something. But I don't think it matters, anyway. It's this guy that's important.'

We turned our attention back to the helix-man.

'It's confirmation, isn't it, Maggie?' said Bernard. 'Proof that someone knew, thousands of years ago, about the existence of genetics?'

'Maybe,' said Maggie.

'That someone played God with us?' I asked. In the excitement of the implications, all my doubts fell away. 'That someone put the missing link into our ancestors?'

'That's what I don't know,' said Bernard. 'But here's my theory.' He pointed to the lowest of the three forms, the one with the streaming hair. 'Here's us, right? Mankind. Created by the helix-man, perhaps. We're sitting at the foot of the mountain and the helix-man is up here in his flying saucer.'

Suddenly we were all babbling at once.

'Flying saucer?'

'You mean he's from another planet?'

'Spaceman?'

Even Sandy was engaged. The only one of us who wasn't, who shook her head in stunned disbelief, was Tina.

'It's possible,' said Bernard.

I pointed to the wavy line. 'I get it, now. This is the clouds, and he's floating above them.'

'And this is a really high mountain,' said Sandy. 'Poking right out above the clouds.'

Bernard was thrilled by our response.

'Exactly! That's exactly what I think. See the helmet?'

I saw it. The bubbly thing: a space helmet.

'A lot of countries have myths about people who come from the skies, or beyond the seas. There are Inca carvings of people in helmets like this. What do you think?'

'I think you're jumping to ridiculous conclusions,' said Tina. But the rest of us, like a gathering of new religious converts, ignored her.

'So who's this guy, then?' said Maggie. 'This ape-man?'

'I don't know,' said Bernard. 'But I have a hunch. He's up above the cloud line, so he's high. Somewhere very high. Get it?'

No one got it.

Bernard encouraged us anxiously. 'No bright ideas?'

Loki put a paw on the bottom of the print. 'Watery-wet-man,' she said.

'That's right,' I said. 'And don't you dare drip on him again!'

Bernard was getting edgy. 'What does he remind you of?'

I stared at the hairy figure and tried not to laugh. I knew what it reminded me of, but I wasn't about to say it.

'No one?' said Bernard. 'Nothing?'

It was like being back at school and trying to

44

hold in the giggles. Suddenly, I couldn't contain myself any longer, and I burst out laughing.

'What?' said Bernard. 'What is it?'

'Nothing,' I spluttered, my giggles gaining momentum. 'It's nothing.'

'It is!' said Bernard. 'What have you seen?'

Sandy was laughing now as well, just because I was, and then Tina joined in, and Danny.

'Please tell us,' Bernard pleaded. 'Let us share the joke. I won't be offended.'

I could barely find breath to speak. 'It looks like . . .' I gasped, ' . . .it looks like . . .'

'Like what? Looks like what?'

The words exploded out of my mouth. 'The abominable snowman!'

The others, even Maggie, fell about the place laughing. But Bernard's eyes lit up.

'Yesss!' he hissed, as though I had just scored a winning goal. 'Yes, yes, yes!'

7

We stopped laughing and watched Bernard as he scooped up the photographs and stuffed them back into their folder. He grinned at me, his face flushed with excitement.

'Someone else had to see it,' he said. 'You have no idea how important that was to me. Even if I had gone, I might always have doubted . . .'

'Just a minute,' said Maggie. 'Gone where?'

Bernard seemed surprised by the question. 'To find them, of course.'

'Find who?'

'Well, the yeti first, I suppose. And then, who knows? Maybe the helix-man himself?'

Maggie shook her head in disbelief. 'Has the sun got to you, Bernard? Have you gone mad?'

'Of course I haven't!'

'But the yeti doesn't exist!'

'Who says it doesn't?'

'I don't know how many expeditions have gone looking for it. They've all failed. Everyone knows by now that there's no such thing.'

'They most certainly don't!' said Bernard. 'Loads of people have seen it.'

'Like who?'

'Villagers. Sherpas. Climbers. Shipton took a photograph of a footprint.'

'Not of a yeti, though, did he? No one has, have they?'

'So what? What does that prove?'

'Come on, now, children,' said Tina. 'Stop squabbling. Kiss and make up.'

Maggie and Bernard looked acutely embarrassed.

'Sorry,' said Bernard. 'It's just . . .' For some reason he turned to me, as though I was a reliable ally. 'What if he does exist? A living remnant of our fore-runners? Think of what we could learn about ourselves. I mean, does he have the missing link gene or doesn't he? All we'd need would be a drop of blood or a hair or a toenail to have the whole genetic code. You never know what we might find out.'

I nodded obligingly. It was difficult to deny that kind of enthusiasm.

'What have we got to lose, anyway?' he went on. 'We can fix up *The Privateer* and stock her up again. Want to come?'

'Definitely.'

'Great. Colin? Tina?'

He didn't mention Sandy. She said nothing, but I could feel the tension in the air above my head, and I turned to look at her. Glaring at her father, she stood up and went out of the room.

Her departure brought everyone down to earth. Maggie shook her head.

'Bernard, you can't do this. We've been breaking our backs keeping Fourth World afloat while you were away. You can't just breeze in and take what you want and leave again.'

I caught a glimpse of something in Bernard's eye; something hard and angry. I recognised it from myself in the days when I lived at home with my mother and Maurice. It was the look I must have had when I was refused something that I wanted; something I believed, however unreasonably, that I was entitled to. I turned towards Maggie. She was watching him as well, with an anxious expression. But when I looked back at Bernard, his eyes were soft and sheepish.

'You're right,' he said. 'We should all sleep on it. Talk it over in the morning.'

8

I puzzled myself dizzy over that photo of the rock carving. Having no alternative theory, I had to agree with Bernard's interpretation of the evidence. It was a wonderfully exciting idea; that we might be descended, however distantly, from a race that originated in outer space. But as far as I could see, it brought us no closer to who they were, or why they came here in the first place. Nothing in the picture indicated that they would ever come back, or that our real home was somewhere among the stars.

I kept searching for significance. A momentous discovery like that ought to have changed my life, but it hadn't. Wherever we originated, I was still human, and still faced with the everyday choices, and lack of choices, in my life.

Things in the outside world had changed a lot since we had arrived in Scotland. The oil crisis was over or, at least, there were supplies of fuel coming into the country. But the damage that had been done by those weeks had not been repaired, and might never be. The bombing and burning of wells in the gulf had done irreparable damage to the environment but, despite that, anyone who could afford the hugely inflated prices was still burning fuel as though there was no tomorrow.

Many, however, couldn't. The consumer economy had collapsed. Thousands of businesses had gone bust, and only the biggest multi-nationals had managed to take up where they left off. Despite the reopening of the coal mines and the increased demand for agricultural labour, there was massive unemployment. Millions of people lost not only their livelihood, but all they owned as well; even their homes. The state, unable to support such numbers, was becoming increasingly repressive in quashing the resulting civil unrest. Police and army numbers rocketed. In response, desperate individuals turned to desperate means. The more law-abiding ones tried to form communities based upon subsistence agriculture; places like Fourth World, but without the advantages that Maggie's independent wealth created. The others, those less willing or able to embark upon such a labour-intensive life, joined the growing number of paramilitary groups springing up all over Europe.

These bands, sometimes numbering hundreds, had no political agendas. They were heavily armed and completely ruthless. No one was safe from their attacks, and even in Fourth World we lived in anxiety. I don't know how many nights I had lain awake, listening to the dogs barking in the distant darkness, wondering if we had been discovered at last.

There were no such disturbances that night, but I still couldn't sleep. My heart was travelling on ahead of me to the high Himalayas. Yeti or no yeti, I wanted to go.

I had been at Fourth World for more than five months, now, altogether. When the public transport systems began to function again, Danny and I had returned to Ireland. I'd had it in my mind that he mightn't stay there, but it didn't occur to me that I mightn't, either.

But everything was so changed, not least, me. The electronic pleasures that had sedated me in the past were anathema to me now. Everything that I did in Fourth World had a clearly visible purpose. School had become meaningless, particularly since the world for which we were being prepared no longer existed.

To my surprise, neither my mother nor my step-father objected when I asked if I could go back to Scotland. They couldn't deny the astonishing improvement in Danny, and if I'm to be honest, they must have seen a dramatic change in me as well. Like everyone else, they were afraid. Society was no longer secure and predictable. No one could anticipate when and where the next crisis would emerge. Danny and I were as likely to grow up safely in Fourth World as anywhere.

It was just as well they didn't know I would soon be heading for Tibet.

Outside my window the light from the kitchen lit up the trees. Someone was still up. I turned over again and tried to sleep, but it was no good. The white, shining mountains crowded my imagination and made my heart race.

I was still awake when my little friend Klaus, the pink mouse, made his rounds. First I heard the tiny drum-roll of his feet as he charged across the floor, then the faint rustle as he navigated the great soft sea of my quilt.

'Who's still up, Klaus?' I asked.

'Mother and Father,' he said. 'Yattering away in the kitchen.'

'What are they talking about?'

'Very private, very private. They shut all the dogs in the scullery. I nearly got ate by that hellhound of yours trying to get through!'

The mention of Loki gave me a sense of unease, even more than was usual. I tried to ignore it.

'But what were they saying? Don't tell me you didn't eavesdrop?'

I knew for certain that Klaus had no scruples. If it hadn't been for him, I would never have seen the inside of Maggie's forbidden lab. And if I hadn't, I might have left Fourth World without ever learning its secrets.

'Boring old stuff,' said Klaus. 'Domestic.'

'What kind of domestic?'

'All the work needed to keep the place going,' said Klaus, in a fair imitation of Maggie's voice. 'Who's supposed to do it?'

'Was that all?'

Now Klaus mimicked Bernard's broad Yorkshire accent. 'But if we had always thought like that, put security above all else, we would never have done what we did.'

'That's true.' Maggie again. 'But now we have responsibilities. We can't just abandon them.'

'I get the gist of it,' I said to Klaus. It didn't sound good. I could see both sides of the argument. It wouldn't be fair to Maggie if Bernard went off exploring again, particularly with the new danger of the armed mobs. But what I wouldn't give to see the Himalayas.

Klaus and I chatted for a bit longer, and then he went off scavenging again. It must have been very late because soon afterwards I heard Danny come in from his night's fishing and thump along the landing on his way to bed. But the trees still glowed with the light from downstairs.

I drifted off into a fantasy of the mountains, and somewhere along the line it became a dream, of huge footprints in the virgin snows. They led straight up into the high peaks and beyond; across the dark skies and in among the stars.

9

Breakfast in Fourth World was always a communal affair. Everyone except Danny, who usually slept all morning after his nightly excursions, would meet in the kitchen to discuss the day's plans. Maggie was always the first to get up, and then Sandy, who did the milking. But that morning was an exception.

There was no one in the kitchen when I went down except for Tina.

'Where is everyone?'

Tina shrugged. 'Sandy's up, I think. The dogs are out.'

'Maybe we should put on the porridge?'

We grew our own oats on the farm and the flakes in the big, steel bin were coarse and fresh. I usually had the job of preparing them the night before, but yesterday's excitement had made me forget.

I sat at the table, sifting through the oats for stray husks and pieces of grit. 'Do you think he'll go?'

'Who?' said Tina. 'Captain Haddock? He's a few tunes short of an album, if you ask me.'

'Maybe,' I said.

'I mean, he finds some old bit of a cartoon in the jungle and thinks he's found the secrets of the universe.'

'It is weird, though. You have to admit it. The double helix and all.'

'It just looked like a squiggle to me,' said Tina. 'It could have been anything. My friend Ronan used to say some of the carvings at the old Celtic sites in Ireland were star maps. It's like everyone thinks they've found God's graffiti, you know?'

I poured the picked-over oats into the pan and took it to the sink.

'What was that about graffiti?' said Bernard, at the kitchen door. He was barefoot, and wearing Maggie's dressing gown. His hair was all messed up and he had a soft, relaxed expression. I turned away to hide a smirk. He did look a lot like Captain Haddock.

'Nothing,' Tina was saying. 'Memories of old Dublin.'

Maggie came in, washed and dressed; her usual, energetic self. She opened the range and threw in some logs, then clacked away at the riddler until she was surrounded by a cloud of fine ashes. I plonked the heavy pot on top of the firebox and it hissed gently.

'Right,' said Maggie. 'Breakfast first. Then we all get together for a meeting.'

When Danny was finally persuaded to get out of bed, we all gathered in the sitting room.

Maggie wasted no time, but started to speak while the rest of us got ourselves settled.

'Bernard and I stayed up for most of the night, discussing what to do next,' she said. 'Not least our responsibilities towards what we have created here at Fourth World. I have to admit that it's been a strain since Bernard and Colin went away. It's been a lot easier to run the place since you three came,' – she looked at Tina and Danny and me, – 'but I still feel I carry more than my share of the responsibility.'

She paused and I glanced over at Sandy, who was rubbing at something on the palm of her hand with the other thumb. Some bit of dirt, I supposed, but there was more to the action than that. It was covering some painful emotion; I was sure of it. Maggie should have mentioned her, of all of us. It was she who worked hardest and longest, and had the greatest commitment to Fourth World.

Maggie took a deep breath and continued. 'But there was something else we talked about as well, and that was the spirit of discovery.'

My heart leapt. I knew, more or less, where her words were leading.

'Bernard and I have both followed our stars. If we hadn't, none of us would be here today.'

Sandy was still rubbing at her palm. Sometimes I wondered whether she was as enchanted by the results of the genetic experiments as her parents were. She had amazing qualities, it was true. She had speed and grace and the phenomenal strength that her frog genes supplied. But she was a prisoner of Fourth World. Her impossibly skinny frame, her stringy muscles, her taut, cadaverous features would create too much attention in the outside world. That was why she hadn't been allowed to go to Africa with Bernard. That was why, I realised, she wouldn't be allowed to go to Tibet, either.

Maggie was still speaking. 'Last night, I realised that my place is here. I'm doing what I want to do; producing new strains of animal and caring for the ones that have already been born. For the moment, at least, there is nowhere I would rather be.'

She paused and looked at Bernard and there was a sadness in her face that troubled me. It was almost a look of defeat.

'In my ideal world,' she went on, 'Bernard would be beside me, following up his work in the lab and helping me to run the place. But unfortunately, that isn't his ideal world.'

For one panicky moment I wondered whether this was a dispute and whether we would all be called upon to vote. Much as I loved Maggie, much as I hated her distress, I knew that my heart wasn't with her this time.

But a vote wasn't on the agenda.

'I can't keep him here,' said Maggie. 'Nor would I want to, if it meant that he had to give up the research that means so much to him.' She managed to smile despite her sorrow, and I thought it was the most heroic speech I had ever heard. 'So *The Privateer* will be setting sail again in a short while,' she finished up. 'Heading for the Bay of Bengal.'

10

Now it was my turn to make a winning goal response. I punched the air with my fist. 'Yess!'

Danny laughed delightedly. Colin grinned and hugged his dad. Tina widened her eyes and screwed her temple with a forefinger. And Sandy, poor Sandy, turned her back on us all and stared out of the window.

'So,' said Bernard, his wonky teeth bared in a broad grin. 'We have a bit of organizing to do.'

'I'm going,' said Colin.

'Me too,' said Danny. 'Out on the big sea!'

'Not me,' said Tina. 'No more sleeping rough for me. You're stark raving, the lot of you.'

Sandy turned back towards us. Her face was a grim mask of determination. 'I'm going,' she said.

Maggie got up and slipped an arm around her shoulders. 'Oh, Sandy,' she said. 'I don't think so, sweetheart.'

In a sudden, dangerous fury, Sandy shook her off. 'I don't care what you say! I've had enough of being the freak, the dairy-maid, the dung-shoveller. Whether you like it or not, I'm going!'

She crossed the room in two springy strides and stormed out, slamming the door behind her. There was a long, awkward silence. Then Bernard sighed.

'I'll talk to her later,' he said. Then he turned to me. 'What about you, Christie?'

I opened my mouth to speak, but as I did so the unease that I had experienced the previous night suddenly landed four-square on my heart.

'I . . . I can't.'

'Why not?' said Bernard.

'Loki,' I said. 'Who'll look after Loki?'

11

Two days later, Maggie and Tina set out early. They had arranged to hire a pair of heavy draft horses from a nearby farmer who had been breeding them for years because he loved them, and now that fuel was so highly priced, found that they were worth their weight in gold. The rest of us, with the exception of Sandy, walked down along the glen to the sea. Loki came with us, and Oggy and Titch flanked her closely as we skirted Bettyhill, to make sure that she kept her mouth shut.

I knew nothing at all about boats, but the moment I set eyes upon *The Privateer* I fell in love with her. She danced on the choppy seas, tugging this way and that at her moorings as if impatient to be off again. High above her, gliding in wide, graceful sweeps, Albert was keeping watch. I waved. He dipped his wings, then turned away and settled on a Northerly breeze which carried him far out to sea.

The tender was a rickety affair and we had to bail out several inches of water before we could set out. Loki kept jumping in and splashing about, snapping at imaginary fish, getting in everyone's way. She stood in the prow as we rowed out, except when I took a turn at the oars. Then she sat under the bench and egged me on, saying 'Hayfoot, strawfoot, me hearties.'

Closer to, *The Privateer* didn't look quite so elegant. She was badly in need of a coat of paint, and some of the boards on deck were spongy. There was a split in her mizzen mast and a big chunk missing from the bowsprit. Bits of the rigging were knotted and frayed, and two of the cabin windows were smashed.

Loki was ecstatic. As we cleared out the stuffy galley and rolled up the smelly bedding, she raced around the boat, her claws a constant clatter on the wooden deck.

'Starboard-pirates!' she panted. 'Cross-and-skullbones! Belay!'

I was on edge, afraid that she might damage something or fling herself overboard, but Bernard laughed himself silly and grabbed at her tail every time she went rocketing past.

When everything was lashed down and ship-shape Bernard put up just enough of the patched and tattered mainsail to propel the boat gently along the coast. Loki stood with her front paws on the bow-rail, gulping the salt wind, and for a while Bernard stood beside her, his hand on her head.

As we approached the harbour we spotted Maggie and Tina backing the horses and trailer down the slipway. We dropped sail and Bernard took the tiller from Colin and sculled slowly in.

It took a fair bit of orchestrating with ropes and poles to settle *The Privateer* above the trailer. Loki hauled on lines with her teeth and raced frantically from bow to stern, barking outlandish orders. 'Hard-a-starlight bow-wow! Scupper-me-timbers!'

Two fishermen came to admire the boat and help with the manoeuvring, and Oggy and Titch hustled Loki below decks. To my relief, she stayed there without a sound while we finished positioning the boat. After that we took down the heavy masts and lashed them securely on the deck, while the tide slowly lowered *The Privateer* on to the trailer. There was a last bit of man-handling to fit her tight and snug and tie her down, and then she was ready to go.

Colin and Danny stayed on board for the ride. The horses leaned into their harness and boat and trailer began to inch up the slipway. Soon they were out on the road and heading for Fourth World, with Colin and Danny waving from the deck high above.

Bernard and I took a short-cut home with the dogs; across the fields and into the glen. We walked in silence for a while, and then Bernard said, 'I'd like to have you along, Christie, when we set out again.'

'I'd love to come,' I said. 'But you can see the problem.'

'I suppose I can,' said Bernard. He watched Loki as she hunted up and down the hill-sides, snapping at brambles and barking at birds. 'I have to admit she's a bit of a loose cannon. But I'm prepared to put up with her if you are.'

'On the boat?' I said. 'You mean she could come?'

'If that's the price for having you along.'

My heart soared up among the bubbling larks. I skipped a few steps, then turned, laughing, back to Bernard. 'That's the price all right,' I said. 'Love me, love my dog.'

PART THREE

1

Bernard and Maggie spent a lot of time together over the weeks that followed. They went for long walks and sat up until the early hours most nights, talking in the kitchen. For nearly a week they disappeared into the lab, coming out only to eat and sleep.

'Catching up on things,' Maggie said. But when I asked her what sort of things, she didn't answer, but smiled in an infuriatingly mysterious way.

They went off on supply trips as well, with Tony and the cart, trying to gather all the things that would be needed to refit *The Privateer*. It was quite a list when they came to write it down. A new mizzen mast and bowsprit, glass for the windows, boards for the deck; several new sails, and all the bits and pieces that I didn't yet understand. None of those things was going to be easy to find; we all knew that. Boats, like horses, had shot up in value since the fuel crisis, and everything to do with them was at a premium. But Maggie's inheritance seemed to be holding up well. There was still plenty of money and Bernard was confident that they would be able to get what they needed.

In the meantime, Danny and I set to work on the boat. We scraped off barnacles and scrubbed off grime and sanded the paint-work right down. It was brutal work, but Danny was patient and tireless, and my enthusiasm tapped reserves of stamina that I never knew I had.

Our absence from the garden made more work for the others. Maggie and Bernard had talked to Sandy. They had, it seemed, persuaded her that she couldn't come with us, but she still felt aggrieved and refused to take on any of the extra work. So Tina, who normally spent her time minding and educating the young animals, was posted on garden duty instead. Colin was drafted in to help her, but he had a great gift for conserving his own energy, and Tina was soon a frazzled wreck, trying to keep up with everything that needed to be done. It made me feel guilty and sometimes, in the long summer evenings, I would do a stint of weeding or digging. But my priority was *The Privateer*. When we'd cleaned her up from stem to stern we primed and undercoated and glossed and glossed again, until she gleamed like polished shoes in the sun. It took me two days to freshen up her name with gold lettering, but I made a perfect job of it; not a drop of paint out of place. I don't know what it is about boats, but they're not like cars or houses. They definitely have a personality, maybe even a soul. I swear that when we had finished that job on her paint-work, *The Privateer* felt as good as she looked.

Sandy did her work quietly and efficiently, as always. She turned up, a little sulkily, for meals. Other than that I rarely saw her. But one morning I cut my thumb on a screwdriver and went into the kitchen to get a plaster. Sandy was in there, straining curds through a cheesecloth.

I was dripping blood all over the place.

'Keep clear of the cheese!'

'Thanks for the sympathy,' I said, fumbling one-handed at the drawer in the table.

Sandy stopped what she was doing and came over to help. She tracked down the plasters and, after several attempts, succeeded in getting one to stick. I sat beside the range, watching the blood oozing through the pink fabric, and she went back to the cheese.

'I hardly ever see you these days,' I said.

Sandy said nothing.

'Are you still mad? About not being allowed to come?'

'Wouldn't you be?' she said.

'I suppose I would. Maybe Bernard will change his mind?'

'You have to be joking,' she said. 'He hates me, can't you see that? He always has. Always will.'

Somewhere deep down, I knew it wasn't true. Whatever was behind Bernard's cool attitude towards his daughter, it wasn't hatred. But I could well understand why she felt the way she did.

'His little experiment didn't turn out the way he hoped, did it?' she went on. 'Oh, it worked, all right. A good combination of human and frog. But no one expected that I'd wind up looking like something out of a horror story. I'm hardly Daddy's little angel, am I?'

'You don't look like something out of a horror story!'

Sandy finished pouring and hung the heavy curds above the pot of whey to finish draining. 'There's no point denying it, Christie. How could anybody possibly love someone who looks like me?'

'Well, hang on a minute. Sandy. That doesn't follow at all. Parents always . . . I mean . . . You don't look that bad . . .'

I was making a mess of it, I knew. She didn't even wait until I had finished, but wiped off the work-top and went to the door.

'I don't care,' she said. 'I'll show him, one day. That he can't just pretend I don't exist.'

The door closed behind her. I was left staring at my bloody plaster and feeling totally helpless.

2

Bit by bit *The Privateer's* requirements were met. Maggie and Bernard's forays produced gallons of diesel, coils and rolls and twists of ropes, rattling bags and buckets of fairleads and cleats and clips. They acquired a second-hand bowsprit and a huge beam of Scot's Pine from which Bernard proposed to hew a new mast. And they bought a small, pot-bellied stove to replace the primus, because the company that made the bottled gas for it had been one of the casualties of the oil crisis.

Only the problem of the sails remained to be solved. There was no way we could carry enough diesel to take us half-way round the world and back, even if we could afford to buy it. So the sails had to be a hundred per cent reliable. The trouble was, Maggie and Bernard hadn't found anyone who was prepared to sell them any; new or old. The best they'd been able to do was to buy a few scraps of sailcloth in two different colours.

So, while Bernard chiselled and pared and planed the new mast, I took a crash course in sewing from Maggie and set out to patch up the sails. It was slow and boring work, and I moved myself into the sitting room, where I could play some of Maggie's books on tape. Loki joined me there, content, for some reason, to listen along for hour after tedious hour. Her favourite, which she clearly recognised, was Moby Dick. We sat through it twice; she snuffling and twitching, me cutting and stitching.

The jib sails were in good condition, and some of the others needed only minor repairs. But the mainsail was in tatters. It had already been patched several times, and huge areas of it were ripped and rotten. I ran out of sailcloth long before it was finished, and had to augment it with a New Zealand rug that belonged to Tony and a new pair of denim jeans that Maggie had stashed away against future needs. By the time I had finished, the mainsail was at least six different colours.

'We'll have to rename her,' said Bernard.

'*Rainbow Warrior*,' said Tina.

'*Patchwork Pirate*,' said Colin.

'*Princess Pansy*,' said Sandy, sourly.

Whatever Bernard and Maggie had been doing in the lab was finished. They joined us, and for two more days we all worked flat out, replacing rotten boards and rigging, fitting the new stove, repairing the broken windows. The day after that, we decided to try everything out. We took out the old bowsprit and slotted in the new one, then manhandled the mizzen mast, golden with new varnish, up on to the deck. Bernard had done a fine job. The base fitted snugly into its housing and the bolts slid smoothly home. The boom fastened tight and secure.

We stood back and surveyed our work. *The Privateer* looked like a million dollars. Above our heads the whole sky was travelling east, making me feel as if we were already moving, heading out into the Atlantic on our way to another world. I couldn't wait. Nor could Loki, it seemed.

'Cast-away!' she commanded to no one in particular. 'Man-the-booty!'

Tina came aboard with a kettle of tea and Colin followed her up the ladder with milk and mugs. Then, while we were toasting the new mast, Sandy arrived on board. One standing jump, twelve feet up, and she was in our midst. I envied her that power. I wished that people could see her; people beyond the confines of Fourth World. I wished she could see the amazement and admiration on their faces as they watched her, and hear their astonished gasps. It wasn't fair that she had to stay here, imprisoned through no fault of her own.

She declined the tea, hopped on to the roof of the cabin, and sat with her long, skinny legs folded under her.

'When do we sail?' she said.

For a long time no one answered. Then Maggie said, with forced cheer, 'Well. I suppose they'll be off any day, now.'

'I'm going,' said Sandy.

Bernard leaned against the cabin and examined the silicone seal on the new window. 'We talked about this, Sandy. I thought you understood.'

'I'll stay out of sight,' said Sandy. 'I'll stay down below whenever there are people around.'

'But we won't be aboard all the time,' said Bernard. 'We'll have to get off when we get there. And people would . . .'

'What?' Sandy snapped. 'What would people do? Stare? I don't care!'

'It could be worse than that, sweetheart. We've been through all this. If we attract the wrong kind of attention we could be in all sorts of trouble.'

'I don't care,' said Sandy again. 'I'm going this time, do you hear me? I'm not being left behind again.'

'Let's talk about it later, eh?' said Bernard.

'No,' said Sandy. 'There's nothing more to talk about. I'm on the lowest rung in this place. The dogs have more freedom than I have. I'm sick to death of being treated like a slave.'

There was another long silence. The shine on *The Privateer* seemed like a cruel kind of vanity, and above us the grey sky was hurrying now, as though we had embarrassed it.

'I'm sorry,' said Bernard at last. 'I wish things were different.'

'You've made that perfectly clear,' said Sandy. She got to her feet and, with one enormous leap, left the boat and vanished among the trees.

3

By the following morning, Sandy still hadn't returned. The excitement of departure evaporated and was replaced by growing concern.

'She'll be back,' said Maggie, over breakfast. 'You lot just carry on, you hear? Get your gear and provisions packed.'

I waited for Bernard to protest, but he said nothing. I spoke instead.

'We can't leave you here like this. Sandy could be anywhere. We have to find her.'

'The horses are booked for tomorrow,' said Maggie. 'I can't change that now. Whatever else happens, *The Privateer* has an appointment to keep with the tide.'

It should have been a great day, but instead we dragged through the hours, sorting out socks, shaking out sleeping bags, searching for shoes. We put everything inside the hall door as we packed it, alarmed at the accumulating piles. There were strings of onions and garlic, kilner-jars of strawberries and plums and pears, beet-root and peas and beans. There were sacks of oats and wheels of cheese, buckets of eggs, drums of salt and butter. There were heaps of pots and pans and plates, barrels of water and bottles of oil, stacks of maps and charts, atlases and books, crates of tools and flares and cameras, drifts of bedding and life-jackets. By mid-afternoon the hall was impassable, and I couldn't imagine how we could possibly get all that stuff on board *The Privateer*. But there was still more to come. Before we were ready to start loading, Bernard had added two inflatable dinghies, a box of lamps and torches and batteries, and two heavy bags which he said were full of things to barter in India and Nepal.

'In case we can't change money,' he said. 'Or money isn't worth anything any more.'

It was happening here already, to some extent, as the economy broke down. People valued money less; goods and foodstuffs more. There was no knowing what condition the Indian economy might be in.

We stopped for a late lunch and Maggie joined us, looking tired and worried. She had spent most of the day searching for Sandy.

'Nothing,' she said. 'The dogs couldn't help, either. The way she moves, she doesn't leave a scent trail.'

'No sign, no sign, no sign,' said Hushy, who was perched on top of the cabinets. He thought as clearly as any of the creatures in Fourth World, but repetition seemed to be hard-wired into his brain, and Tina's best efforts to educate him out of it had come to nothing. 'I've been out, been out with Darling since dawn, since dawn, since dawn. If she was moving we would have, we would have, we would have seen her, her, her, her.'

'I'm sure she'll turn up,' said Maggie. 'Where could she go, after all?'

But I could tell by her face that she wasn't as sure as she said she was. None of us were.

We loaded the firewood first, filling the hull through trap-doors in the galley and the living quarters. After that the rest of us fetched and carried while Bernard stowed everything away. I couldn't believe how efficiently he used the available space. There was a place for everything. By the time we had finished all that stuff that had accumulated in the hall seemed to have vanished.

It would have given us a great sense of satisfaction if it hadn't been for Sandy. There was still no sign of her. Before it got dark, we all went out and looked for her, but we came back home disappointed.

There was nothing more to be done. Reluctantly, we peeled off and made our way to bed. But everyone knew that there wouldn't be much sleeping done that night.

4

When Maggie and Tina arrived with the horses the next morning, Bernard and Danny and I went aboard *The Privateer* to take down the masts for the trip to the shore. From the deck I could see a small pile of firewood at the edge of the yard, underneath one of the trees. I hadn't noticed it before, and I was about to mention it when I remembered that the hold was already packed tight with logs. Even if we had forgotten some, there was no way we could fit any more on board.

The launch went as smoothly as anyone could have wished. The horses were careful and wise and waited with infinite patience for the tide to come in and lift the boat clear of the trailer. In the meantime, we put up the masts and made everything ready. As *The Privateer* floated free we all sent up a cheer, and Loki leapt aboard from the harbour wall, terrified of being left behind.

The horses were up to their bellies in water, and Maggie led them out.

'Get aboard, the rest of you,' she said. 'Be gone.'

'We'll just take her out to the mooring,' said Bernard. 'Shouldn't be long.'

'You will not take her out to the mooring,' said Maggie, in a tone of such authority that it sent Roxy scuttling for cover. 'You have a voyage to undertake. There's no point in delaying it.'

'But Sandy . . .' Bernard began.

'Tina and I have talked about that. We came up with an interesting theory, didn't we?'

Tina nodded. 'She wants to stop you going. She's found a perfect way to do it.'

I wasn't convinced. 'It's possible . . .' I said.

'It's probable,' said Maggie. 'I'd be willing to bet that she'll turn up within a few hours, once she realises her scheme has failed.'

Bernard opened his mouth to say something, but Maggie stepped up close to him and took his hand. 'Go, Bernard,' she said, gently. 'Before I change my mind.'

They hugged each other long and hard, and then there were hugs all round. I hadn't realised until that moment how much I was going to miss Tina, and I tried not to let it show as I kissed her goodbye.

'We'll be back soon,' I said. 'You'll see.'

'Bring me a yeti,' she said.

Bernard grabbed one of *The Privateer's* mooring lines and hauled her in against the pier wall. 'All aboard!'

79

We needed no second bidding. Danny went first, then Colin, then me.

'All the men,' said Maggie. 'How did that come about?'

'Sure you don't want to come?' said Bernard.

Maggie laughed and shook her head. Bernard hugged her again, then turned to cast off the head-rope. But at the last moment he stopped and straightened up again.

'Hold on a minute,' he said. 'Where's Titch?'

Colin wanted to go back for her, and I suspect that Bernard did, too.

'She didn't know we were leaving,' he said. 'She'll be heart-broken if we go without her.'

'We'll explain,' said Maggie, taking the rope from Bernard's hand and pushing him aboard. 'She'll get over it.'

'I've forgotten my toothbrush!' said Danny.

'So have I,' I said. 'And my pyjamas.'

'You'll live,' said Maggie, throwing the rope out over the widening gap and on to the deck.

'Hushy!' I shouted, spotting him on a stack of empty lobster-pots. He fluttered over, and Roxy appeared from behind a pile of nets and leapt aboard. Suddenly there was no more time for anything. The boat was in danger of running aground against the slipway and Colin rushed to get a pole to push her head around. Bernard grabbed a halyard and began to hoist the heavy mainsail.

Danny and I ran over to help him. We were

no sailors, and before we had even cleared the little harbour Danny had got his finger pinched in a fairlead and I had got knocked down by the mizzen boom. But somehow we survived and a few minutes later *The Privateer* was under full sail and heading out to sea.

5

The water wasn't rough but it was choppy, and a few whitecaps broke up the copper-green expanse of the surface. *The Privateer* bounded ahead, like an eager horse taking hold of the bit, and as we left the land behind us I learned the first rudiments of sailing.

We were barely ten miles out from land when two things happened. Firstly, we were spotted by Albert, who came soaring in from the west, buzzed over our heads, and came around again to land on the mast.

'Off again?' he called down.

'We certainly are,' said Bernard, grinning with delight.

'Need a look-out man?'

'We certainly do. But an albatross would be even better.'

The humour was lost on Albert. He stood looking down for a long, long time, and eventually he said, 'Lots of you this time.'

I remembered that he had trouble with numbers. 'Seven of us,' I said.

'I can see that,' said Albert. 'Seven people.'

'Not seven people. Four people.'

'I can see that,' said Albert again. 'Four people take away Roxy and Hushy and that mad black thing. That makes seven, doesn't it?'

I tried not to laugh at him. 'Very good, Albert.'

He waggled his shoulders like a Samurai warrior, then spread his huge wings and dropped on to the wind. A moment later he was a tiny speck against the drifting clouds. Innumerate he might be, but there wasn't much else that escaped him.

The second thing that happened was that I began to feel sick. At first I thought I was just a bit queasy, worn out by too much excitement. But before long I was kneeling over the weatherboard, expelling the contents of my stomach into the ocean. My head was reeling, and I couldn't look sideways without heaving, even when there was nothing left to bring up.

Bernard put a strong arm around my shoulders and Loki wedged herself between his thigh and mine.

'Not got your sea legs yet?' said Bernard.

'Seal eggs?' I said, hoping they might be some kind of magical cure.

'You'll just have to ride it out, Christie. You might be more comfortable below.'

If I could get there, that was. Either the whole world was lurching, or there was an earthquake happening inside my head.

'Take your time,' said Bernard. 'Want a hand?'

'I think I've got some,' I said. 'I'm just not sure where they are.'

Loki preceded me to the hatch. She fell head-first down the ladder, but it didn't inconvenience her at all. Since her recovery from the accident she seemed to be made of rubber; impervious to any kind of pain. As if to prove the point, she scrabbled back up the ladder, turned round, and proceeded to do exactly the same thing again.

As I tried to manoeuvre myself into position I wondered if her way mightn't be worth something after all. At least if I knocked myself out I wouldn't feel sick any more.

Slowly, carefully, I edged backwards down the ladder. Long before I got to the bottom I became aware of a terrible scraping sound. I thought we were running aground. I thought we had met with an iceberg and were about to follow *The Titanic* to the bottom. I thought my head was full of rats, trying to scratch their way out through my ears.

But it was none of those things. It was Loki, scrabbling at the trap door in the floor.

'Oh, please,' I said, resisting another fit of retching. 'What are you doing?'

'Boing,' said Loki.

'Boing?'

'Spring-thingummy,' she said, scrabbling even harder with her claws.

'There's nothing there, Loki. Only firewood.'

'Bouncymajig!'

I never shouted at her, never. But I was just too ill to cope with her. 'Just stop!'

She flattened her ears against her skull and slunk on her belly beneath the table.

I was too ill to be sorry, too ill to make it to my berth, too ill to get a slop-bucket from the galley. I sprawled on the nearest bench and, reaching underneath it, located a big, plastic first-aid kit. A few moments later its contents were rolling about on the floor and the box was beginning to fill up with unspeakable gastric secretions.

It could have been minutes or hours or days later that Danny came down and sat on the bench beside me.

'Poor Christie,' he said. 'Poor Christie.'

Roxy had followed him down. My world was going round and round and round, and somewhere in the middle of it, the fox was sniffing around the trap door, just where Loki had been scratching.

'What is it, Roxy?' said Danny. 'Something down there?'

Roxy cast a sly glance at us. 'No, no. Nothing down there. Nothing at all.'

He joined Loki under the table and scratched at his ear with a hind paw. Loki sighed deeply.

'Cook-wood,' she said. 'Boing.'

I closed my eyes and spun gently away from them all, down into my own, private hell.

Just once, I came back to reality. It was dark, and the world was still revolving, and I could hear the faint sound of a trickle of water coming from below the floor.

'We're sinking,' I said. But there was no one around to hear me and there wasn't a thing I could do.

For the whole of the next day the sea-sickness gripped me. Danny fretted, hovering over me half the day, but Bernard was unconcerned.

'You'll be over it soon,' he said. 'And when it's over it's over. You'll never look back.'

He was right. The next morning I was groggy and weak, but the sky and the sea were back where they were supposed to be, and the boat was safely between them. Whatever seal eggs were, I had found them.

PART FOUR

1

A week later, I was as comfortable aboard the boat as if I had been born there. The sailing had been patchy, with winds that were not quite as co-operative as Bernard would have liked, but we had made a reasonable amount of progress, and had long since stopped looking back and started looking forwards.

I had just taken my turn to sleep, after doing an early morning watch with Colin, and had woken to the smell of cooking fish. *The Privateer* was bowling along through the waves, lifting and dropping on the swell, making good headway by the feel of it.

It was Danny frying the fish, bracing himself with one arm against the tilting and rolling of the boat. Loki was beside him, managing, despite sliding backwards and forwards on the floor, to monitor the fish with constant care.

'Did you have to go deep to get them?' I asked Danny.

'Not too deep,' he said. 'You coming next time?'

'Not a chance.'

The pan was crammed with whiting fillets,

dipped in eggs and oats and crisping nicely. I was still surprised by the transformation that Danny had undergone since he discovered his genetic inheritance. Now that Maggie had helped him relearn how to breathe; to keep his oxygen intake steady, his perpetual giddiness was gone. He would never be famous for his manual dexterity, but he had attained a fair degree of competence in most areas of life.

'How are we doing?' I asked him.

'Not bad. Making good headway. Problem with the radio, though. Doesn't seem to be working at all.'

Carefully, he turned the fish over in the pan and shook it around.

'Ready now,' he said.

I turned to go and call the others, and walked straight into someone who was blocking the gangway. My mind flipped and double-flipped, because the person who was standing there wasn't on the boat. Or shouldn't have been.

'Sandy!' I gasped.

'Hi, Christie,' she said, cheerfully.

Danny and I said nothing; just stood staring, our jaws practically scraping the ground.

But Loki didn't seem in the slightest bit surprised. 'Bouncy bouncy,' she said. 'Boing.'

2

Bernard was spitting nails over the dead radio when I went up to fetch him, but he forgot about it when he heard what I had to tell him. He looked over my shoulder at Sandy, who was hanging back, glaring at him defiantly. I don't know what I expected. I somehow thought that he would prove Sandy wrong by his reaction; that he would be delighted to see her safe and sound; that some sort of glorious reunion would occur and be followed by all that happy-ever-after stuff. And when he first saw her, I think it was a flush of relief that passed across his face. But it soon vanished, replaced by some darker emotion.

'What on earth do you think you're playing at?' he said.

Colin adjusted the self-steering gear, and over breakfast we had our first council-at-sea. Sandy was adamant that she wasn't going back.

'If you turn the boat round I'll throw myself overboard,' she said.

'Keel-haul,' said Loki. 'Clap-in-irons.'

'Just try it, wonky-bonce,' said Sandy.

Bernard shook his head. 'It's not that I mind you being aboard, Sandy. But how will your mother manage without you?'

'She's got her precious Tina. And the two of us managed for months when you and Colin first went away.'

'I know that. But it's different now. Maggie is . . .' He stopped.

'Maggie is what?'

'Nothing. It doesn't matter. But she'll be frantic, wondering where you are.'

'We'll have to go back,' I said. 'Even if it's just to let her know you're safe.'

Bernard said nothing, but that dark look was in his eyes again and it was clear that he was beginning to be annoyed by the situation.

'Mercury,' said Loki.

'I'm not going back,' said Sandy.

'Wingy-messenger,' said Loki.

Hushy got her gist. 'I could go, I could go and tell Maggie, Maggie, Maggie. I mightn't be able to, able to find my way back, though, though, though. I'd have to stay there, I'd have to stay there.'

'What about Albert?' said Colin. 'He could go.'

'We'd be taking a chance with other shipping,' said Bernard. 'And with the weather, now that the radio's out. But I suppose we could risk it.'

Everyone agreed that it was the best plan, and we went up on deck and signalled to Albert. He settled on the main mast and we had to shout above the wind and the slapping of the sails to make ourselves heard. He agreed to go, and when we were sure he had understood what the message was, I made the mistake of asking him how long it would take him.

'How long?' he said.

'Yes. How long?'

'Eight?' he said. 'Nine? Ten?'

'Ten what?'

He gave an embarrassed shrug and shifted from one foot to the other.

'Halibut?' he said. 'Herring?'

'That's fine, Albert,' said Bernard. 'Just come back as quickly as you can, all right?'

The bird spread his enormous wings and the wind knocked him backwards from the mast. My heart missed a beat, but he twisted in mid-air, circled the boat, then sailed away to the north-east. We watched him until he was out of sight, and in all that time he didn't once beat his wings, but rode the sea winds as though they were his to command.

Back down in the living quarters, Loki had been clearing the table. The scraps were all gone, and the butter, and the last of the fresh milk we had brought. Most of the plates were on the floor and had been licked clean.

'You're impossible,' I said to her.

'Red-conspirator,' she said, looking pointedly into the corner where Roxy was sitting, trying to be invisible.

'Are you in on this too?' I said.

'Me?' said Roxy.

'And while we're on the subject, you knew Sandy was down in the hull, didn't you?'

Roxy didn't try to deny it.

'So why didn't you tell anyone, eh?'

Roxy drew himself up to his full height and puffed out his white chest.

'I'm a fox,' he said, proudly. 'If someone has gone to ground, you don't go and grass on them, see?'

3

Albert never made it to Fourth World. He had barely been gone for an hour when he met weather conditions that made him turn back.

Bernard and I were on deck and Danny was out fishing when Albert located us and dropped out of the skies.

He didn't land, this time, but drifted over our heads, calling to us as he went.

'Drop sail! Front coming in!'

Bernard opened the hatch and roared for Colin and Sandy to come up. Then he raced to let off the self-steering gear, and I began to take down the sails. Within moments we were battling against high winds, and the waves, which had borne us along without complaint for so many miles, began to turn nasty and try to climb up on to the deck.

The Privateer pitched and reared and plunged. Colin fought his way forward and hauled in the jib while Sandy and I battled with sheets and halyards, hanging out of them one minute, letting them go the next as the deck bucked wildly beneath us. But we succeeded in getting the foresail and the ketch sail down just in time.

If we hadn't, *The Privateer* would have been hit side on by the wind and gone straight to the bottom.

Bernard was in the wheelhouse. He had started the engine and was turning *The Privateer* to run before the storm. Colin joined him there, and Sandy was trying to open the hatch to go down below. But my concerns were for Loki. She must have been on deck all the time; I just hadn't seen her until now. The boat was climbing the waves and dropping into the troughs, and the deck was like a see-saw. Loki was skidding wildly, scrabbling with her claws for a purchase that she just couldn't find. And I was too busy trying to hang on myself to be able to help her.

The boat reared up again, and Loki slid backwards along the deck, hitting the lip of the aft hatch just as Sandy closed it behind her. Then, as the boat entered another trough, she slid forward again and collided with the main mast.

Bernard opened the cabin door and shouted to me. 'Get in here!'

But I couldn't, not without Loki. The waves were breaking all over the deck and she was sliding on the wet surface. Down below I could hear things clattering around in the galley. Then I saw Bernard, making his way towards me, clinging on to the main boom. A monstrous sea tilted us over, brought our faces within inches of the heaving water. It was blackish, yellowish; the colour of an angry old bruise. And Loki was sliding towards it, all four legs back-pedalling uselessly. As she was about to roll over the weatherboard, Bernard found a free hand and grabbed her by the tail. She yelped, but as the boat rolled back and we rose towards the scowling skies, she came with us.

As *The Privateer* plunged down again, Bernard let go of the boom and allowed himself, with Loki in tow, to slither across the deck. The cabin wall stopped him and he managed to get a handhold before we pitched again. He kicked at the door, and an instant later Colin opened it and hauled Loki inside.

Bernard took a couple of breaths and then beckoned me over. I had both arms wrapped tightly around the mizzen mast. My chance came as the boat dropped into another hollow, but somehow I couldn't let go. The wind hurled stinging rain into my face like a handful of gravel. The boat leaned back, and for an instant I was submerged as a wave broke over the deck.

'Christie!' Bernard yelled.

The Privateer was plunging again. Still I couldn't let go.

And then I realised why. 'Danny!' I screamed. 'Where's Danny?'

I felt Bernard's hand grip my ankle, and the next time the deck reared up he slid across to me, crashing into my knees. He grabbed a stay and pulled himself up until his face was close to mine. His hair and beard were drenched, pasted against his skin.

'Danny,' I said again.

He shook his head. We were already dropping into the next trough.

'Now!' he said, prising one of my arms free.

I let go. The back of the boat was so high that I heard the engine whine as the propeller came clear of the water, and we were almost in free-fall when we slammed into the cabin. It should have hurt, but it didn't, and Bernard moved quickly, hauling at the door.

The deck was awash and a substantial wave came in with us as we slithered inside. But the door fell to behind us and Colin latched it tight. We struggled to our feet in the small space.

If anything it was even more terrifying in there. Loki was tumbling around like a pinball, trying to glue herself to the floor. I did my best to wedge myself into a corner, but it was almost impossible to stay upright.

Bernard took the wheel from Colin, and a fierce light seemed to gleam in his eyes as he fought to hold *The Privateer*'s head steady. It was almost as though he was enjoying himself.

'At least it's blowing us in the right direction,' he said.

'The right direction?' I snapped. 'How can you say that? Don't you realise that Danny's still out there somewhere?'

Bernard said nothing, but kept his eyes firmly fixed upon the boiling seas ahead. A fleeting image came into my head, of another captain, on another boat.

'Bernard?' I said.

There was no answer. He had shut me and my concerns out, as effectively as if he had slammed a door between us.

4

For nine or ten hours the storm raged on. None of us had escaped without nasty bruises, and by the time it was safe to stand up and move away from whatever we had been clinging on to our limbs were stiff as boards from the protracted effort.

As soon as it was safe we went out on deck. The breeze was still strong and there was a heavy swell, but the dawn was breaking and we could already see brighter skies coming in from the west.

We all spread out around the boat, looking across the turbulent grey waters and calling, hoping for some sign of Danny. We were on the point of giving up when a large, flat fish flew up out of the sea and landed with a heavy slap on the fore-deck. A moment later it was followed by Danny, propelling himself high enough out of the water to catch hold of the weatherboard and then climb over.

He was as pink as a boiled lobster, glowing with health and grinning broadly. We crowded around him, effusive in our relief, but he waved our worries aside.

'I was in the safest place to be,' he said. 'It was you lot up on the surface who were in trouble!'

Breakfast was a precarious but delicious affair. Danny and Colin were on the galley shift and, while they washed up, the rest of us went up on deck to take a closer look at the work of the storm.

It could have been a lot worse. There were bits of debris around; seaweed, driftwood, a dead guillemot which made us all concerned for Albert's safety. The mizzen boom had broken loose at some stage, and its volent swinging had twisted the clamp on the mast and splintered the wood. But Bernard said it hadn't bitten too deep and he could patch up the wounds without much trouble. What mattered was that the metal had held and the hinge hadn't buckled. Two or three stays had snapped as well, but there were replacements in the engine compartment.

'We were lucky,' said Bernard. 'If the storm had gone on for much longer we might have lost the new mast.'

'Bye-bye, yeti,' said Sandy.

'Isn't it bye-bye anyway?' I said.

'Why should it be?' said Bernard.

'I don't know.' Somehow I had assumed that such terror and violence would be enough to turn anyone back. 'I just thought . . .Without the radio or anything . . .'

Bernard bent to unfasten one of the broken stays. 'Got cold feet, Christie?'

'No,' I lied. 'But what if Albert didn't make it back to tell Maggie about Sandy?'

Bernard continued with what he was doing and didn't look up. I waited until it became apparent that he wasn't going to give me an answer. It appeared that the subject was closed.

The wind was still blowing from the best possible quarter for us, and Bernard was keen to make the most of it. We hoisted all the canvas except for the ketch sail, which we couldn't use while Bernard was working on that boom. But even without it, we began to make great headway. Colin showed me how to set the wind-vane, which regulated the self-steering mechanism and enabled the crew to take a break from time to time. Then a school of dolphins came to swim with us, and Danny leapt in to join them. The rest of us leaned out over the weatherboard and reached for their blunt noses as they jumped clear of the water.

The Privateer sent up a fine spray to cool the sweat on our faces as she plunged forward through the waves. I swear she was enjoying every minute of it, showing us what she could do when the conditions were really in her favour. Before long, Bernard finished his repairs and the last sail was hoisted. I could feel the difference it made as the wind filled it, and for the first time I began to sense that I could enjoy this sailing business, if more of it was as satisfying as this.

We were still going strong when Albert flew in from the west. He was amused by our fears for him and told us that he had simply flown out around the front and followed in behind it until he found us again.

'You must explain this genetic business to me some time,' he said to Bernard. 'Because it seems to me that creatures who are unable to fly must be an accident of nature.'

As I watched him soar off for a look at the surrounding seas, I was half inclined to agree.

5

The storm had pulled everybody together, but as the emergency receded into the past, the strain between Bernard and Sandy became apparent again. I don't believe they ever spoke about it. It just lay around the boat like a web of invisible trip-wires, and everyone had to think and speak with unfailing care.

There were good things, though, as well. Like the moment when, after all the days and weeks of struggling to understand, I suddenly realised that I was developing an instinct for the wind and the way the sails should be rigged to make the most of it. And after that I was so consumed with learning more that I lost track of where we were, and was amazed when Bernard told me that we had already left France far behind and were travelling past the distant shores of Spain and Portugal.

I learnt to change course when Albert warned of the presence of a ship or a sand-bank. I learnt how to tack and beat against an unfavourable wind. I learnt which knots and hitches to use where, and which ones never to use anywhere. And as I gathered knowledge we continued to cover the miles until we entered the waters off the coast of mainland Africa.

Danny took a limited interest in *The Privateer*. He joined us for meals and he took his turn on watch at night, but as the Atlantic grew clearer and warmer he spent less and less of his time on board.

Nobody minded, really. He was bringing us more fish than we could eat, and we had plenty of hands on deck. But his love for the ocean worried me. There were times when he got dreamy and remote and didn't hear when people were talking to him. I found myself working hard to keep in touch with him and I realised one night, with a chill, that his dolphin side seemed to be winning out over his human side.

I waited for an opportunity to speak to him about it. It came one evening soon afterwards. We were moving slowly through a drizzling mist and Albert was close to the boat, quartering the vicinity carefully. Colin was in the wheelhouse and, for the moment at least, there was nothing that needed to be done. I sat beneath the tarpaulin that we used to catch rainwater, and waited for Danny to come aboard.

It was nearly dark when he arrived, trailing a string of lobsters tied together with seaweed.

'Talk to me, Danny,' I said.

'Course I will, Crinkly,' he said. But for a long time I couldn't think of what to say and we were both silent, gazing into the mist. Eventually I made a stab at it.

'You wouldn't ever leave us, Danny, would you? To live at sea, I mean. For ever.'

'Of course not,' he said. 'I don't know how to sleep in the sea. I don't know how the dolphins do it.'

'Is that the only reason?'

The question seemed to shock him and I wondered if he had realised how distant he was becoming.

'You're my brother,' he said.

'Not your real brother.'

'Colin is, though, and Sandy's my sister. You're my family, Christie. How could I leave you?'

But even as he said it his gaze returned to the sea, and I could sense the longing in his heart.

The mist had thickened and it seemed as though water was everywhere; under us, around us, over us. The remnants of the breeze had dropped. The sails were slack. *The Privateer*, I realised, was becalmed.

'Do you hear anything?' said Danny.

I listened. The only sounds were the drip and trickle of the gathered droplets running from the tarpaulin into the tank.

'No. Do you?'

Danny glanced at me, then shook his head. The mist was so thick now that we could barely see the surface of the water.

'Do you ever get the feeling you're being watched?' said Danny.

I thought about it. I got all kinds of creepy feelings, but that wasn't one of them. I shook my head. 'Do you?'

He nodded. 'Under the water, sometimes.'

'You probably are being watched down there. All those weird fishes and things.'

He didn't answer, but I could tell by the way he looked at me that it wasn't what he meant.

6

Throughout the whole of the next day *The Privateer* stood still, slack-sailed and helpless, exactly where the winds had abandoned her. The mist sat on top of us like a cloud that had fallen out of the sky and couldn't find its way back home again.

'Why don't we use the engine?' I asked Bernard.

'This could last for days,' he said, irritably. 'We can't risk using the fuel.'

While we waited for the wind I did a few repairs on the mainsail, where some of my stitching had proved weak. Colin replaced a frayed halyard, and Bernard set Sandy to scrubbing the deck. It provoked a moment of tension, and I thought we might have a minor mutiny on our hands, but Sandy relented and channelled her resentment into frenzied activity. By lunchtime we had finished with everything that needed to be done, and when Danny came back from the sea we collared him for a game of Monopoly. Bernard declined to play. He said he couldn't stand the game; it brought out the worst in people. But Colin said that he was just restless and grumpy because he preferred fighting a good storm to being becalmed.

Loki wanted to play, though, and couldn't be dissuaded from pouncing on the dice every time they were rolled. In the end we had to put her out, to prowl the deck with Bernard.

The game passed the time away, but Bernard had been right. Sandy won hands down, and the rest of us wound up hating her. We tried a game of rummy to calm things down, but when she started winning that as well the rest of us threw in the towel.

In the afternoon, while Colin and I slept, Danny taught Sandy to swim. She took to it, he told us, like a frog to water and had such a powerful kick that she could almost keep up with him.

Colin and I got up for dinner. By the time we had eaten and cleared up the galley I was beginning to understand Bernard's frustration. The mist was making me claustrophobic, and it reminded me of a time, long ago, when I had been playing hide and seek with a group of pals. I had hidden in the back of my mother's wardrobe, and some bright spark had decided that it would be more fun to lock me in than to find me.

It had been OK to begin with; even a relief from the nervous excitement of the game. But after a while I began to worry. What if no one came to let me out? I could be there forever.

I felt a bit like that now.

There was no reason, after all, to believe that the mist was ever going to lift.

7

It was my turn to take the midnight watch. I had done it three or four times before, but then we had been under sail, and Bernard or Colin had always stayed out on deck with me, just in case. This time I was on my own.

Somewhere above the clouds there must have been a moon, because the mist glowed dimly around me and I could see well enough to move around the boat. The whole world was eerily quiet. Even Loki, who was with me, seemed awed by the ghostly white silence.

I walked softly around the deck, not because there was anything much to watch for on such a night, but because it was too spooky to be keeping still. Loki padded behind me, poking her nose into dark corners and peering out at the invisible sea.

The hours passed like a murky dream, full of imaginings, empty of logic. No foghorns sounded, no bows loomed out of the gloom. But once, from somewhere behind me, came the soft plop of some unknown creature breaking the surface. I leant over the weather-board and watched the ripples run in widening rings until the water forgot that they had ever been there.

Everything was silent, but Loki's ears were pricked and she was cocking her head from side to side, as though she was hearing things.

'What is it, girl?' I said.

'Angel-sing,' she said.

The words sent a shiver through me. I listened hard for a long time, but there was nothing; not the slightest sound. Then Loki let out a long, thin howl which sent icicles shooting through my brain.

'Do you have to do that?' I said. 'Do you have to try and freak me out?'

Loki cringed and wagged her tail apologetically. 'Sing-sing,' she said, cocking her head again. 'Sirenspeak.'

I paced the deck, and if Loki heard anything more she didn't mention it. It was getting on for four o'clock, the end of my watch, when Danny appeared on the deck.

'I'll take over, Chrysalis,' he said.

'If you like.'

'I couldn't sleep.' He sat down and swung his legs over the side. There were a lot of things that he was allowed to do and we weren't. Sitting on the weatherboard was one. Not wearing a life-jacket was another.

I went below but Loki stayed on deck, still listening out for her 'angels' perhaps. Colin stirred in his sleep, as though expecting my call, but there was no need to wake him with Danny on watch. I sank luxuriously into my bunk. At times like this it reminded me of how my mother's arms had once been; snug and warm and safe from a world that was sometimes too big and confusing. I forgot about the gloom and the silence and the size of the ocean beyond our lost cloud, and my dreams welcomed me among them like old friends.

But I wasn't to be allowed to stay there for long.

8

I was woken by Loki's frenetic barking coming from the deck above. By the time I got to the ladder, Roxy, Bernard and Colin were already queuing up on it, and Hushy shot out through the hatch the instant it opened.

Sandy was behind me as I started up, but she sprang past me and on to the deck. I was the last to emerge, but it was to me that Loki ran in her panic.

'What is it?' I said. 'What happened?'

She just kept on barking, racing ahead of me to the starboard bow where I had last seen Danny. There she stopped and peered out over the edge into the dark water.

'Slithery-swimmery,' she said, breathlessly. 'Danny down-a-down.'

'He's just gone swimming, Loki. He does that all the time.'

'I don't believe you've woken us all up for this,' said Sandy, leaping across the deck and down the hatch in one go. Loki looked up at me intently, pleading for understanding.

'Swimmeryman,' she said.

'Yes, yes. He's a swimmeryman. We all know that, you stupid dog!'

Loki turned in three tight circles. I walked away and she came after me, putting herself between me and the hatch. I tried to step past her but, to my complete amazement, she grabbed my ankle between her teeth and began to drag me across the deck.

'Ow! Loki, get off!'

Bernard came to my rescue and pulled her away, but she broke free of him and returned to the rail.

'Watery-fish-man!' she babbled. 'Danny down-a-down-down.'

'Yes, Loki,' I said, exasperated. 'Danny down-a-down. He's gone fishing. Get it?'

The only response Loki made was to bite me on the ankle again.

Bernard shook her hard and locked her into the wheelhouse. Colin went back to bed, but I was too unsettled to sleep. I stayed out on deck with Bernard.

'What am I going to do about her?' I asked him.

He shrugged. 'Let me see that leg.'

He lit a torch and shone it on to my ankle. There were several red marks, but the skin wasn't broken.

'Why did she do that?' I found that I wasn't far from tears. If Loki was losing her senses what would I do?

'There's no telling with a head injury,' said

Bernard. 'It ought to have stabilised by now, but maybe it hasn't. She's young, after all. Her hormones could be kicking in and stirring things up in there.'

My tears spilled over. I couldn't stop them. 'Do you think she's going mad?'

Bernard put an arm around my shoulders and gave me a reassuring squeeze. 'We won't do anything drastic,' he said. 'We'll keep an eye on her and see how things go. All right?'

9

Loki greeted me with her usual daft exuberance when I went out on deck the next morning. I was thrilled to see that the mist had gone and I could feel a brisk wind tugging at my shirt sleeves and rattling *The Privateer*'s rigging. But the booms were swinging loose. We weren't moving.

'We're waiting for Danny,' said Sandy. She was wrapped in a towel and had clearly been out for a swim herself; looking for him, perhaps.

'He's bound to pop up in a minute,' I said.

He didn't, though. *The Privateer* lolled on the swell, ready for the off, but we were as stuck as if we were still becalmed.

There was no fish for breakfast, either, and it worried me slightly, because Danny was reliable about providing our meals. So we ate the last of the Fourth World eggs and lingered as long as we could over the clearing-up. After that there was nothing left to do except wait.

Albert and Hushy scoured the seas for Danny but saw neither hide nor hair of him. Even so, it wasn't until noon came and went that I really began to worry. And when I started sifting possibilities in my mind, it occurred to me that there might, after all, have been method in Loki's madness.

When no one else was around, I called her over to the starboard bow where Danny had last been seen.

'Where's Danny, Loki?' I said. 'Tell me what happened to Danny.'

But Bernard's punishment had taken effect. Whatever misdemeanour Loki was supposed to have committed, she wasn't about to risk doing it again. She crawled away on her belly and lay beside the wheelhouse door.

'Ignoble beast!' she grumbled. 'Bad dog!'

The previous days of hanging around were nothing compared to this one. Every minute that passed felt more like an hour. *The Privateer* was restless, longing to run before the wind, and Bernard's frustration created a razor-wire fence all around him that none of us dared to breach.

Colin was the best of us; a sailor right down to his toenails. He took down the tarpaulin when it started to flap and got a load of washing done and, as evening drew in, he cooked Danny's lobsters even though no one felt much like eating them.

By the time we had finished, darkness had fallen. We hung around for ages, as though going to sleep would somehow make it less likely that Danny would come back. In the end, Bernard ordered us off to bed and, one by one, we drifted towards our bunks.

I was woken from a troubled sleep in the early hours of the morning by an argument taking place on the deck above my head. I could hear Bernard's voice, low and menacing, and Sandy's, more strident, more clearly audible.

'You can't do this,' she was saying. 'It's inhuman!'

I could feel the movement of the boat as she barrelled along over the waves. We were under way.

Bernard spoke again. I couldn't hear what he was saying, but I understood the tone of voice. It reminded me of the time before, when he had left Danny behind during the storm, and the image I had seen in my mind's eye returned to me, much more clearly. Bernard no longer brought Captain Haddock to mind. It was Captain Ahab up there on deck, standing at the wheel.

Maybe it was all right. After all, Danny had found us the last time we had sailed on without him. But this was different, somehow. This time there was no storm. This time there must have been something else that prevented him from returning to the ship.

For a few days I kept a close watch on the seas around the boat, half expecting Danny to pop up, as he had done before. But as time went by my watching became automatic and desultory, and eventually the day came when the truth dawned. Danny wasn't going to return.

During the days and weeks that followed, I was so numbed by the grief and shock of his disappearance that it didn't really matter to me where I was. The work of sailing *The Privateer* kept my hands busy, and the increased responsibility that I was given occupied my mind. The trade winds were blowing against us for much of the journey, and we seemed to be engaged in a slow, running battle with them. By the time we rounded the Cape of Good Hope and sailed into the Indian Ocean, I could have given a comprehensive course on tacking and beating.

We met with more bad weather as well and once, when I was up on watch on my own, we were hit by a sudden squall. It took the others a while to come and help, but in the meantime, Bernard said, the action I took probably saved the boat.

But the pleasure and pride I might have taken in my new-found skills were absent. My heart had stayed behind, somewhere around the line of twenty-five degrees latitude. At night, in my restless dreams, I trawled the sea-bed there, looking for my brother.

PART FIVE

1

As we were sailing on down the coast of Africa, Maggie and Tina were getting close to the end of their tethers. The summer was damp and mild, and everything in the gardens was ripening at once. Day after day was spent picking the fruit and vegetables; blanching and freezing, pickling and bottling, until all the freezers were full and there were no more bottles or jars left to use.

Maggie was determined that nothing should be wasted. She made a deal with one of her regular traders to take all the surplus produce and pay her in fish; some fresh, some preserved in a local smokehouse. Now that they no longer had Danny, it was a good deal for them.

But the endless work was taking its toll. There were animals to be cared for, potatoes to be sprayed, winter crops to be sown, buildings to be repaired and maintained. Tina noticed that Maggie's energy was not up to its usual level. She tired more easily and her appetite was poor. The lab-work slipped; she fell behind with her programme of research and, slowly but certainly, she was losing heart.

Tina did her best to buttress her flagging spirits, but she was struggling against the odds. There were things that she could remedy, but the greatest burden on Maggie's heart could never be lifted by anyone. Not as long as her only daughter remained missing.

Time after time the two of them sifted through the probabilities, but the only solutions to the disappearance that they could come up with were bad ones. Sandy had met with an accident of some kind, or been kidnapped and kept as a freak for someone's amusement. Neither of them mentioned it, but the paramilitaries were always there at the backs of their minds. What would people like that do to Sandy if they stumbled across her?

To make matters worse, Titch fell into a dreadful decline as soon as the others had gone. She believed that Bernard and Colin had left her deliberately, and nothing any of the others said could convince her it wasn't true. She pined away to nothing and, eventually, weakened by fasting, she contracted pneumonia. All Maggie's efforts to save her failed.

She was the first of the talking animals to have died. To Maggie, already grieving for Sandy, it seemed like some terrible omen; a sign that her world had gone wrong. She began to have doubts about all she had done, and Tina's best efforts could not persuade her that there was any merit at all in her life's achievements.

But still she worked on because work was in

her nature. And because, although she didn't say it, she was terrified of what might happen to her if ever she was to stop.

2

Bernard's plan was to moor *The Privateer* somewhere off the coast of Orissa and to lead us overland across the north-east corner of India to Nepal. But it was a lot easier in theory than it was in practice. The entire coast was lined with villages and swarming with fishing boats, and even Albert failed to locate a safe and secluded spot to moor.

Bernard spent a lot of time at the port side of the boat, peering through his binoculars. 'There are so many people!' he said.

'This is India,' said Sandy. 'I could have told you that there were lots of people and I've never before set foot outside Bettyhill!'

Still searching, we wound up getting a lot closer to the mouth of the Hooghly River than we had intended to. We got so close, in fact, that Albert resigned his post and returned to sea. There was, he said, no need for him to report on the state of shipping. We could see it perfectly well for ourselves.

We could, too. Apart from the little fishing boats, there were cargo boats, some big and some small, and quite a number of ferries crowded with people. We could see coast-guard patrols as well and something that looked like a gun-boat. Bernard's nerve failed, but as we were swinging around to turn back, a small, scruffy sailing dinghy came speeding towards us across the bay.

To avoid a collision, we slackened off the sails. *The Privateer* slowed to a crawl, but the little boat had changed direction and still seemed to be on a collision course.

'Hold off!' Bernard yelled.

At the last possible moment, the dinghy hove to and nestled alongside *The Privateer* like a duckling beside its mother. Bernard's eyes were popping out of their sockets at the skill of the sailors. There were two of them, both boys, and they looked closer to Colin's age than to mine.

'Do you need a pilot, sir?' One of them called.

'A pilot?'

'For the Hooghly River, sir. Very wily river. Very dangerous.'

'No, thanks,' said Bernard.

But the boys didn't make any move to go. 'My name is Vijay, sir,' the same boy said. 'I have very good connections. You want to sell dollars? Sterling?'

'Certainly not,' said Bernard.

'Are you selling any whiskey? Cigarettes?'

'We're just looking for a safe mooring,' I called, before Bernard's frantic dig in the ribs could stop me.

'Ah,' said the young sailor. 'You come this way. Very safe mooring. Very cheap.'

'You idiot,' said Bernard as the little boat drifted away. 'You can't trust these people!'

'Why not?' I said. 'I thought they were very nice.'

'Of course they were very nice,' said Bernard. 'Con-men always are very nice. That's how they con people!'

I shrugged. 'It doesn't seem to me as if we have many options.'

We followed the boys for a few miles down the coast and in through the narrow mouth of a deep, sheltered bay. It was like many of the other places we had seen, with houses standing above the high tide line and small fishing boats pulled up on to the beach. The boys came alongside and told us to wait, then sent their little craft speeding towards the shore. At the very last minute they dropped the sail and swung her around, in the equivalent of a slick, hand-brake turn, and Vijay jumped into the shallows and ran up the beach.

A few minutes later they were back and they led us to where a cracked plastic water-can bobbed on the surface.

'Here is good mooring, sir,' said Vijay. 'One hundred rupees a day. Five hundred rupees a week. Sterling or dollars is OK, too.'

'How do we know it's safe?' said Bernard.

'Motilal will guard it, sir.' Vijay pointed to his

quiet friend, who stood up now in the swaying dinghy and waved a long, heavy stick.

'Is real lathi, sir. Captured from the police during a strike.'

The boy wasn't much broader than the stick, and it was hard to see what use he would be able to put it to if push came to shove. But Vijay played his trump card.

'Very honest people here, sir. Simple villagers. No one will touch your boat.'

Bernard stared into space for a long moment then sighed in resignation.

'Very well,' he said. 'It's a deal.'

While Vijay secured *The Privateer* to the mooring, we took down the sails and stowed them away below decks. Then we finished packing our rucksacks and, when everything was out on deck, Bernard locked the hatches.

Since we had left the leaky tender behind us in Scotland, we took a lift in on Vijay's little boat. He made no comment as Loki jumped in, and then Roxy, but although Sandy had fashioned a headscarf out of an old night-shirt, it went no way towards fooling Vijay or Motilal. As she climbed down into the dinghy, both of them stepped away from her.

Vijay gasped. 'This is no good,' he said. Motilal muttered something in Bengali and Vijay repeated it in English.

'She is ghost woman. Not welcome here.'

'She's not a ghost woman,' I said.

'She's . . .ill,' said Bernard. 'A wasting sickness.'

'That's why I'm so thin,' said Sandy.

Vijay seemed to relax a little. Bernard pressed home his advantage. 'That's why we're going to Tibet.'

'Tibet?' said Vijay.'

'To see the Dalai Lama,' said Bernard. 'To get his blessing. A cure, perhaps.'

Vijay shook his head suspiciously. 'Dalai Lama is not in Tibet. Dalai Lama is in Ladhak since 1959.'

Bernard was flustered. 'Of course he is. It's another lama I'm talking about. In Kathmandu.'

'Only hippies and bed-bugs in Kathmandu,' said Vijay. 'You go to Monghyr instead. Very great yogi is there. Centre of yogic healing.'

'What a good idea,' said Bernard. 'We'll do that. But we'd better get ashore now, hadn't we?'

The little boat was barely afloat with all the weight in it now, and Motilal's departure for the deck of *The Privateer* made no noticeable difference. Vijay took up the sail and she began to pull sluggishly out across the bay. I sat in the stern and hugged Loki tight to my chest, giving her a quiet lecture about keeping her mouth shut and behaving in a proper manner. She licked my face and made little whiny sounds, but she didn't say anything and I hoped she had got the message.

'You have passports?' asked Vijay. 'Visas?'

'Well,' said Bernard. 'Not exactly.'

I smiled to myself, secretively. For all Bernard's mistrust of the boys, we were the ones who had the most to hide.

3

A crowd of curious children followed us up the
beach as Vijay led us to his mother's house.
Even without Sandy's bizarre appearance we
would have made an odd procession: Bernard
hadn't warned me that it takes as long to find
your land legs as it does to find your sea legs,
and we were all lurching about the place like
drunks.

Vijay's mother had heard the commotion on
the beach and was standing at her door, thrilled
to discover her son at the centre of the
excitement. He introduced her to us as Ruma,
and she invited us warmly to come into her
house. Until, that was, Sandy came close
enough for her face to be seen.

Ruma's jaw dropped and her hands flew to
her mouth in horror. She backed away, and
there was no knowing what might have happened had Vijay not stepped in to save the
situation. A long, fraught conversation followed,
and though none of us understood a word of
Bengali, it was not too difficult to guess what
was being said. The end result was that Ruma
disappeared into her dark little kitchen and the

rest of us were ushered, slightly ignominiously, back out into the sunlight.

We hadn't been given our marching orders, however. Vijay produced a bundle of rush mats, spread them out in the shade of the house and invited us to make ourselves comfortable.

We did, as far as was possible. By now the word of the new arrivals had spread far and wide, and a crowd that would not have shamed a third division football team had gathered. Vijay gave a running commentary, which produced swells of surprised and sympathetic response from the crowd.

Sandy kept her scarf pulled up around her face. If her wishes had been heard, the ground would have opened and swallowed her up, and I would have let it take me as well. Even the dogs seemed subdued by her discomfort. The only one who wasn't, who might almost have been gloating over her misery, was Bernard. Every glance he gave her had the same message imprinted in its expression. 'Don't say you weren't warned.'

Gradually the people tired of the attraction and began to wander off. Some of the children started up a game of cricket down on the beach and, without my noticing, Loki slipped off and joined in. I would have called her back when I realised, but she was proving to be a useful player. She positioned herself at mid-off and fielded every ball that came her way with spectacular speed and precision. As I watched, she made a brilliant mid-air catch, and all the members of the fielding team threw up their arms and roared with delight.

Ruma brought us strong, sweet tea in small cups and a plateful of sticky *ladoos*. As we sipped and nibbled, Vijay explained the local transport situation. He seemed to be very knowledgeable about the complicated road and rail networks, and when he had elicited a confession from Bernard that we were going to Tibet despite the Dalai Lama's absence from it, he offered us various possible routes.

'You're not having any problems with fuel supplies, then?' I asked.

Vijay laughed. 'More than likely. India has constant problems with everything. But we always manage to . . .'

He was interrupted by a commotion as a crowd of small children came racing across the beach. Ruma went forward to meet them and there was a babble of excited chatter. It was all in Bengali, but I caught the occasional English word, like 'leg-spinner' and 'googly'.

Ruma turned to face us. 'They are telling me your dog is speaking to them!' she said.

'She'd better not be,' said Bernard.

Ruma roared with laughter.

'Better not be!' she said and translated for the children, whose voices exploded in a clamour of indignation. I called Loki to me and ordered her to lie down quietly with Roxy. Ruma joined us again, shaking her head fondly.

'Children!' she said. 'Such imagination!'

4

We spent what was left of the day lounging on the beach and re-packing our rucksacks. Ruma cooked us a delicious meal and afterwards she disappeared for half an hour while Sandy and I helped Vijay to wash up at a tap in the back yard.

When Ruma came back she had with her a burka, the long, hide-all garment that the Muslim women wear in public, complete with a veil. Sandy was indignant when it was suggested that she should wear it, but when she recovered from the initial shock she had to admit that it was a good idea. And once she was inside it and had the veil pulled down over her face, it made a brilliant disguise. There was no way anyone could see who or what was underneath.

We slept on the beach that night, out under the open stars. Vijay slept out there with us, and so did a lot of the village children, still infatuated with Loki. I kept her close beside me, though, in case she committed any further indiscretions, and she settled down quickly, worn out by her sporting endeavours.

But I found it harder to sleep, and I could tell that Sandy, lying a few feet away from me, was wide awake and staring into a terrible, lonely darkness.

Bernard's insensitivity to her embarrassment was verging on cruelty. Was Sandy right to suggest that he hated her? Was he indeed an Ahab, so driven by his own obsessions that he had no consideration for anyone else?

And what was it all for, anyway? A piece of information so small that it couldn't even be seen without a special microscope. I could understand Bernard's curiosity about the origin of our species. I shared it myself. But I didn't share his obsessive drive. Whatever we might learn from this expedition, could it really be more important than family? Than life itself?

For the first time it occurred to me that we might all have been wrong to go off so readily with him and to abandon Maggie.

I thought of her now, and of Tina; the two of them slaving away on their own at Fourth World. We ought to have turned back instead of continuing with this wild goose chase. We ought to have told them that Sandy was safe, and that Danny . . .

I tried to break the chain of thought, but it had already brought me too far. Even in her sleep, Loki was aware of the vast tide of emotion that I had kept stemmed for so long, but that was now rising up to engulf me. She woke and licked the tears from my face as the words crashed and tumbled through my defences.

We ought to have told Maggie and Tina that Danny was dead.

PART SIX

1

But on that score, I later learnt, I was wrong.

That last night, as Danny sat on the weather-board of *The Privateer*, he had heard the singing again. Or maybe singing wasn't exactly the right word. It was more like a soft, sweet, sad call that set his emotions askew.

And maybe 'heard' wasn't the right word, either, because the sound was certainly not in the air around him. It seemed to be in his blood or his bones, transferred there by the bulk of the boat. And transmitted, through her, by the sea.

Or by something in it.

Danny saw nothing. Only Loki, as she had tried so hard to explain to me later, saw what it was that emerged from the water and dragged Danny down by the ankle. And before she could react and warn him, he was long gone, far beneath the surface of the sea.

Instinctively, Danny had snatched a deep breath as he went under. He kicked and struggled as hard as he could, but the grip on his leg was like a vice and nothing he could do had any effect on it at all.

Whatever it was that had caught him was heading straight down for the deep. Although he didn't have a dolphin's sonar system, Danny had a strong sixth sense that helped him to orient himself in the darkness of the sea and identify other living things. He had encountered all sorts of weird and wonderful creatures in the deep, but the one that was dragging him now was something outside his experience.

About a hundred metres down, Danny's captor levelled off and began to swim parallel to the surface, away from *The Privateer*. Now Danny could feel the powerful beating of fins creating turbulence in the water beside his head. His panic was depriving him of oxygen, and he began to fear that he would drown before this creature, whatever it was, ever got around to eating him. With a tremendous effort, he bent double and managed to reach his ankle. But what his fingers encountered there sent a swift shock through his blood.

There was no mouth, no teeth, no predator's jaw. The thing that gripped him felt much more like a human hand.

2

Danny tried to prise open the bony fingers, but they were so strong they might have been tree roots. His need for air was becoming desperate and he kicked out again and tried to swim against his captor. To his surprise and relief, the creature slowed its progress and began to rise towards the surface. A moment later, Danny's head was above the sea and, as he drew breath, he whipped around and caught a quick glimpse of what it was that held him.

It was also coming up for air, and it had a dark, whiskery, almost human face.

Then he was dragged under again, and they were speeding away, further and further from the safety of the boat. Since struggling was only making his own life more difficult, Danny gave it up and allowed himself to be towed along like a goose in the jaws of a fox. They stayed closer to the surface this time, and every two or three minutes they rose for air. After a while, Danny noticed that the dawn was breaking and from then on, each time they surfaced, his picture of his kidnapper grew clearer.

In many ways he was very close to a human

being. His eyes were much larger than Danny's, and he had weird, fleshy whiskers around his nose and mouth. Otherwise, his features were those of a young man. His height, or his length, was roughly the same as Danny's, and he had four discernable limbs. His feet, however, were flattened and ribbed like flippers, and from his spine protruded something that seemed to be a dorsal fin.

They travelled on in the same way for about an hour. Several times Danny made attempts to stop their progress, to face the creature above the waves and attempt to communicate. But it didn't respond to his efforts, nor did it catch his eye once.

By the time it was fully light, Danny knew that they were not alone. From time to time he had caught a glimpse of another face rising to the surface as he did, and after the third or fourth time, he realised that it was not always the same face, but several different ones. At a distance, but moving along on a parallel bearing, there were other sea people, both male and female. And as they swam clear of the shifting mists and his view of them became clearer, Danny came to a realisation. All those stories and songs from the past were not just fancies after all. He had been taken prisoner by the merfolk.

For no reason that Danny could see, the little troupe came to a halt and gathered around him, a few feet below the waves. His keeper let go of his ankle at last, allowing him to float up to the welcome air above. He took a few deep breaths and his racing heart began to steady. One by one, other faces appeared, peeping up timidly then slipping back down again. The singing was all around him; the short, eerie phrases passing back and forth between the sea people. Danny knew now that the sounds were their communication and he wished that he could understand.

He went under again, and the others followed him. One by one they approached, their expressions anxious at first, then softening as Danny showed no sign of aggression and permitted the gentle touch of their cold, wiry fingers.

All of a sudden, the sea was full of smiles. The water began to swirl and churn as Danny's new friends showed their delight at his presence. They surged and dodged and dived and leapt with such child-like exuberance that Danny was infected by their mood and joined them in their lithe, subaquatic games.

As he did so, he understood that they had been aware of his existence for a long, long time. He had heard them, far out in the oceans, singing to each other; perhaps to him. He had felt their eyes upon him as he fished from the shore or from the deck of *The Privateer*. Now that he was among them, it seemed to him that he had always known they were there. They somehow had to be, to fill a void that otherwise existed in his world. And as they called their children up from the hidden depths to meet him, Danny came to another conclusion. They had carefully awaited their moment and then, believing the boat to be paralysed, they had made their move. But in dragging him overboard, they hadn't intended to kidnap Danny. As far as they were concerned, he was one of their number and they had at last succeeded in rescuing him.

He knew that he should have returned to *The Privateer*, if only to say goodbye. He knew he was free to do so. But he was afraid that if he left his new friends he would never find them again. For thousands of years they had managed to escape detection; no other species on earth were so expert at keeping hidden from human eyes. So when they regrouped and set out again, Danny went with them. Despite what he had said to me the other evening, he had long suspected that the sea was his natural home. And now he had found his community within it, he was certain.

3

In retrospect, the weeks that followed were an expression of some kind of shared insanity. When I look back at it now, I can't imagine how any of us could have been mad enough to go along with Bernard on that excruciating journey. But we were, and we did, and as each challenge arose we met it, and did our very best not to think about the next one.

We travelled on train carriages that were popping their rivets with the pressure of the humanity packed inside them. We perched on the tops of buses that careered round hairpin bends with drops of a thousand feet or more just inches from their worn tyres. We slunk across borders by night and bribed our way in and out of Kathmandu, where we kitted ourselves up with second-hand climbing gear and stocked up on provisions. Then we set off into the foothills of the Himalayas, blundering through dense forests and plunging through paddy fields in our efforts to escape the notice of prowling policemen.

I don't know what we must have looked like, with Sandy still in purdah and the rest of us bundled up like Arctic explorers. When we did have to pass through a small town or a village, we attracted plenty of attention, but on the whole the Nepalis were accustomed to eccentric trekkers and accorded us more tolerance than we probably deserved.

But the real madness didn't begin until we left the cool green foothills behind us and began to travel through the snows, among the highest mountains on the planet. I don't know how many times I was uncomfortably reminded of my near escape in the blizzard in Scotland, just a year ago. Up there, constantly above six thousand metres, every step was a near escape.

Bernard had plenty of seafaring experience, but none whatsoever of conditions like these. Despite our efficient equipment, we were as ill-prepared for life at that altitude as if we had fallen out of a plane and landed there by accident.

Our faces got sunburnt and frostbitten at the same time. The dogs' paws froze, and we had to construct mittens for them from a spare thermal waistcoat. Bernard got a mild case of snow blindness before he could be persuaded to wear his goggles, and I'm sure that, despite our relatively gradual ascent, we all suffered varying degrees of altitude sickness.

It was a miracle that none of us succumbed. We were utterly helpless up there. If anyone had got seriously ill they would have had it. Even if we'd had a radio or a mobile phone, no helicopter pilot could have flown in there to rescue us, and the knowledge that we were anything up to three weeks' walk away from the nearest road did nothing for my peace of mind.

Progress was agonisingly slow. There was plenty of time for thinking during those gruelling marches. Day after day, hour after hour, I travelled along the same worn-out pathways in my mind. We weren't going to find the yeti. Even if we did, what could we possibly learn? If the yeti had the missing link gene, so what? What else did Bernard expect to find? A spaceship? Little green men doing experiments in an underground complex? I wished I could have been more optimistic. It would have made the journey a lot easier.

On a good day we covered ten miles. On a bad one, we were turned back by unscalable crags and unbridgeable crevasses, or we floundered through snows so deep that it took the day's energy to cover half a mile. But through all of it we were driven on, pushed up to and beyond our pain thresholds, by Bernard's determination to find what he had come to look for.

4

On his own in the sea, Danny had always been guessing and experimenting. But the merpeople knew the sea as only the most ancient of human races know the land, and Danny's underwater education was about to begin in earnest.

The only trappings that any of them wore was a kind of tight belt or cummerbund, woven from a strong, light weed. Its purpose was to hold the few implements that were necessary for the sea people's nomadic existence. Each one of them carried a sharp weapon of some kind, used for spearing larger fish. Harpoons, lost by whalers, were common, and Danny saw all kinds of variations on the theme, some fashioned from natural materials like wood and flint. Others – a poker, a toasting fork, a sharpened billiard cue – had clearly been salvaged from wrecks. There were smaller tools as well; sharp stones or rusting knives, used for collecting shell-fish from the sea bed and splitting them open. Every man, woman and child carried a comb, exquisitely carved out of whalebone, and a privileged few had mirrors, whose previous owners would be unlikely ever to need them again.

Danny never learnt to understand the sing-song speech, nor did he ever learn how the merpeople produced it. But as time went by he devised a system of signals and gestures with which to communicate, on a basic level at least. And for his own sake, he needed to have names for his new friends. The man who had dragged him from *The Privateer*, and who later made him his first weed belt, he came to think of as Weaver. The girl who gave him a flake of stone for a winkle-knife was Molly Malone. And the woman who taught him which of the shell-fish were good and which weren't, became, for some reason, Mrs No-No. The children got mad names; Jinxie and Mo and Mitsy and Digser and Spiffler and Amble. The names were meaningless and their owners would never know them, but they helped Danny to remember who was who, which wasn't always easy in the dim world beneath the waves.

Over the next few days, Danny watched and imitated and learnt a hundred new things. His friends taught him how to find warm underwater currents and how to wash himself with a kind of pumice to get rid of the sea lice which were a persistent irritant to the merpeople and their children. He learnt how to locate flat fish on the sea bed and how to lie in wait for the plump cod on their regular runs. He learnt how to repel sharks with a black ink that the others gathered from a squid-like creature in depths that Danny couldn't reach. But of all the things he needed to know, the one he needed most was proving impossible for him to learn. No matter how he tried, he wasn't able to sleep.

He had observed how his companions managed it, lying beneath the surface and rising every five minutes or so to reach the air and take a breath. The process was as instinctive to them as turning over in bed would be to him. But when he tried it he found he couldn't relax and trust himself, and though he dozed for a few minutes from time to time, the deep sleep that he so badly needed continued to elude him.

He began to make mistakes; to slip behind the others on their hunting expeditions and to see things that weren't there. His nerves were in a constant state of excitement and he became so edgy and distressed that the others began to be wary of him. Although he didn't know exactly what it was that they feared, he got an intimation of it when he blundered close to a drift-net in the fishing lanes, and had to be led hurriedly away by Mrs No-No. He stayed close to her for the rest of the day, and by the time darkness fell it seemed that she had come to understand what his problem was. That night, she linked her arm in his beneath the surface of the sea, so that he rose with her every time she floated up to breathe, and he was finally confident enough to let go of his consciousness and fall into a deep and dreamless sleep.

When he woke in the morning she was gone. Danny didn't know how long he had been managing without her, but it was enough. He had finally learnt to sleep at sea, and after that he knew that he could really do it. He could live, for all of his life if he chose to, out in the depths of the ocean.

5

I don't know how many miles we covered, plodding in single file across the snow. Bernard had maps and compasses, and spent long sessions each morning and evening taking bearings. But where we were heading we had no idea.

None of us had an easy time with the extreme cold. Roxy seemed happiest, once his feet were protected by the down-filled boots. Loki tended to keep herself warm by staying on the move, but she consistently forgot why she was wearing the boots and tried to tear them off at least once a day. Hushy couldn't stand to be out in the open for more than a few minutes at a time, and stayed inside my thermal vest all day, sharing some sort of invisible but extremely itchy parasites with me. To begin with, he would come out from time to time to have a look around, but he soon lost interest in the endless snowy vistas, and contented himself with emerging twice a day, when we cooked up big meals in the tents.

On the whole we didn't have enough breath to do much talking as we went along. Even on level ground, walking through the deep, untrodden snow took all of our available energy. By the time we had pitched our tents in the evening and gone through the exasperating process of cooking a meal and eating it before it froze solid, we were generally too tired to do much more than fall asleep. But one night, as Sandy and I lay top to toe in our sleeping bags, we found each other in the mood for a chat.

'How do you rate our chances, then?' Sandy asked me.

'Of what?' I said. 'Finding the yeti or surviving?'

'Finding the yeti, of course,' she said.

'Nil. And as for ever finding our way out of here, maybe five per cent. What about you?'

'Ah,' she said, knowingly. 'You're beginning to see the truth at last.'

'Truth? What truth?'

She dropped her voice, aware of the thin tent walls and of how close to ours the other tent lay. 'The truth about your precious Bernard,' she said. 'That he's not as reliable as he pretends to be.'

It didn't bear thinking about. Was it possible that Bernard had no more idea of where we were than I did?

Sandy carried on, compounding my anxieties. 'Just because he's an adult doesn't mean he's competent, you know. He's obsessive. Always has been. Completely untrustworthy.'

'Thanks for that,' I said. 'I feel a lot more confident now.'

She laughed, and I realised that she sounded really happy for the first time since the day Bernard and Colin had arrived back into Fourth World. For an instant I wondered if she was beginning to lose her grip.

'I wouldn't mind,' she said.

'You wouldn't mind what?'

'If we didn't make it out of here.'

'Well, I certainly would,' I said.

'Oh, I know we couldn't really survive,' she said. 'I mean, we'd need supplies, and we could all do with a hot bath and a decent night's sleep. But it's great, too, you know? For me, anyway. It's the only time in my life that I haven't had to keep hidden.'

She had stripped off the hated burka the minute we were above the snowline and it was only brought out at night for use as an extra blanket.

'Even when I'm at Fourth World I'm always watching,' she said. 'In case someone comes wandering in from the village or something. But up here ... well ... I'm hardly likely to be seen up here, am I?'

'I don't know,' I said. 'What about the yeti?'

She burst into another fit of the giggles. It was great to hear her laughing. It was, I have to admit, great to hear myself as well.

In the morning, trudging along in Bernard's big footprints, I found it hard to remember what that laughter had felt like. Every day my stamina declined, and it seemed to me now as though I had hardly started walking before I was too tired to walk any further. But whatever Sandy said, I had no choice other than to put my trust in Bernard, so that was what I did. I plodded along in his footprints, day after day after day.

The worst of it was that we found no reason for optimism. As each new snowscape revealed itself to us, Bernard would scan the whole vista as though expecting the yeti to pop out and give us a wave. On several occasions he spotted likely-looking caves or overhangs, and went off, alone or with Colin, to check them out. But he found nothing, not even a footprint. If the yeti was around, he was keeping himself to himself.

6

From watching the others, Danny learned a lot about how to regulate his diet. In warm waters, the merpeople tended to favour fleshy, juicy fish which satisfied thirst as well as hunger. In colder parts they sought out more oily species, to maintain the crucial layer of body fat which kept them warm. On the whole, the merpeople were healthy but their children were as prone to viruses and infections as human children are.

The tribe had medicines, gathered from various aquatic plants and organisms, but sick children need cossetting as well, in the sea just as on the land. And because of that, Danny found a position for himself in the community.

Compared to the other adults, he was a poor hunter and gatherer. He couldn't dive nearly so deep; his eyes were not as good as theirs in deeper waters, and his fingers were far too big and clumsy for some of the more delicate tasks. But as a nurse for ill children, he was without comparison.

He was caring and patient and steady. Since he didn't understand the language he didn't get distressed or irritated, as other adults did, by the children's cries and calls. But Danny had a further advantage over the others. The human body temperature was at least a degree higher than that of the merpeople so, lying curled up in Danny's arms was the equivalent of being wrapped in a warm blanket. His success with their children delighted the community, and conferred upon him a status he had craved until then. He was not only accepted by his marine friends now. He was needed.

PART SEVEN

1

Maggie was woken one morning by a strange conversation taking place on the garage roof outside her window.

'I don't think she'd like it,' said one of the voices.

'Of course she would,' said the other. 'It's a present.'

'I'm sure that she'll be polite about it. But I know for a fact that she doesn't like mackerel.'

'How could anyone not like mackerel?'

Both the voices were familiar. The first one was Oedipus. And the other . . .

Maggie leapt out of bed.

'I'd be happy to take it off your hands,' Oedipus was saying. 'It would save you the embarrassment.'

'It's a present,' said Albert. 'And it's not for you!'

'Albert!' said Maggie, at her bedroom window. 'How wonderful to see you! Are the others back?'

'No,' said Albert. 'They had just arrived in India when I left them.'

'Oh.' Maggie tried to be pleased for them, but she couldn't help feeling disappointed.

'I brought you a present,' said Albert, bending to pick up the mackerel. But it was nowhere to be seen and nor, for some reason, was Oedipus.

Neither Maggie nor Tina would ever forget the emotional mangle they were dragged through that morning. First came the news of Sandy's appearance on board *The Privateer*, which sent their spirits soaring and had Tina racing for the elderflower champagne. But before they had time to celebrate, Albert broke the news about Danny, and their hearts plummeted again.

'He could be all right,' said Tina. 'He could have been picked up by a trawler or found a desert island, or . . .or . . .'

The wild swing of emotions was too much for her, and she burst into a flood of tears. The dogs gathered at her feet, surrounding her with sympathy and warmth. She hugged Oggy tight against her chest.

'Danny's gone,' she sobbed into his fleecy coat. 'Dolphin Danny's gone.'

Albert failed in his take-off attempt from the garage roof, and ended up sprawling on his chin in the drive. He shook himself off and waddled back to Maggie.

'No lift,' he said. 'Now I'm stranded.'

Even though he knew the Fourth World dogs, Albert was terrified of being attacked and

Maggie opened the front door and let him inside.

'What about the roof of the house?' she asked.

Albert agreed, but refused to let Maggie carry him up. It took ages for him to flap and flop his way up the stairs, and even longer to negotiate the steep steps up to the attic. But he made it in the end and, reluctantly, allowed Maggie to help him with a final lift up to the skylight. He was extremely heavy, and he fluttered his wings so hard that he got in his own way. But eventually he burst out, slithered down the steep slates, and was away, back in the arms of his beloved winds.

By the time Maggie came downstairs, Tina had sobbed herself out. She relinquished her hold on Oggy and allowed Maggie to give her a hug. They both stood helplessly for a few minutes, as though they were lost in their own kitchen. Then Maggie said, 'I suppose there's only one thing we can do.'

Tina sighed deeply. 'I know,' she said. 'Keep going. Get on with the work.'

2

Danny's new family were browsing their way gradually northwards. From time to time they encountered other tribes of merpeople, and these meetings were generally friendly, and gave rise to a certain amount of flirting among the opposite sexes. There was, needless to say, a great deal of curiosity about Danny. It seemed that his own people must have communicated his skill with sick children because after a while anxious parents from other groups began to seek him out and bring their little patients to him for attention.

He gave more credit to Mrs No-No's medicines than to his own abilities, but he was undoubtedly selling himself short. From his dolphin kin, Danny had inherited a lightness of heart and an expansive nature that made him generous with his attention and unstintingly kind. To the merpeople, there could be no doubt that their infants benefited from basking in his gentle care. And the results proved them right. He and Mrs No-No made a terrific team, and for a long, long time their success rate ran at a hundred per cent.

Their fame spread far and wide. On one occasion, Danny found himself attending two small infants at the same time, and he was rarely without some little ailing companion, either in his arms or recuperating and swimming at his side.

But the time came when things began to go wrong. Danny and his friends were lying off the northwest coast of Spain, just outside the Bay of Biscay. He was enjoying a rare respite from his nursing duties and was hunting with Molly, trying to run down a tricky little dog shark, when a pair of his younger friends came racing through the water to fetch him.

Mrs No-No was waiting, just below the surface, along with another young merwoman that Danny hadn't met before. She had a child in her arms and Mrs No-No was already examining it. She was clearly concerned and Danny could immediately see why.

Danny guessed that the merpeople matured at about the same rate as humans did, and that the child was five or six years old. She was listless; lolling in her mother's arms and showing no interest whatsoever in her surroundings. Her skin was covered in lesions, showing up angrily red against her mottled grey skin. They were on her head as well, and patches of her hair had fallen out. Even as they watched, more strands broke free and drifted away in the tide.

Mrs No-No glanced at Danny and he understood that, like him, she was out of her depth with this one.

Over the next forty-eight hours, they made every effort to save the little girl. Her mother, clearly not well herself, hovered around the underwater infirmary in a state of acute distress. Mrs No-No administered sea herbs and the powerful medicines that she extracted from urchins and whelks and weeds. Danny held the child close to his chest the whole time, creating a safe warm nest with his cradling arms. When the sun was shining he rose to the surface and held her there, hoping that the warm air might succeed where everything else was failing. But nothing could help her. By the morning of the third day, she lay dead and limp in Danny's arms, and the little tribe gathered around to share her mother's sorrow.

Later, they carried her down to the seabed, covered her over with rocks and left her for the crabs to dispose of. No worse than the worms on land, Danny supposed, but it gave him the creeps all the same.

The child's mother left to rejoin her own people, but Danny's clan stayed in the area for several more days. It wasn't until a trawler passed by that he understood why. His companions dived down to the merchild's grave and guarded it closely as the boat passed above them. They had lived undiscovered for thousands of years, and no risk was too slight to ignore. If the cairn of stones was disturbed by an anchor or a net weight the corpse might be exposed, and though Danny couldn't imagine what the result of such a find might be, the mer-people clearly could.

In the end, the trawler came nowhere near. But while they were waiting and watching, some of the children made an interesting discovery. Among the rocks which were the child's grave, and on the seabed all around it, were an unusual number of dead and dying crabs.

3

Soon after the death of the merchild, some members of the same group came to Danny again with another dying girl. This one also had hair loss, but the lesions were not so apparent. She was even more listless than the first one had been, and it seemed to Danny as he looked into her impassive eyes that her brain must have been affected. She appeared to have no awareness of her environment at all, and none of Danny's efforts to stimulate her had any effect. She lasted for eight hours, and then she died.

Despite these two failures, the same tribe brought another child, an older boy this time. Danny and Mrs No-No did everything in their power to help him, but they had already come to realise that they were helpless against this particular disease, and within a few days the third child also died.

One moonlit night, Danny's people, still making their way northwards, paid a visit to the coastline. It was the first time since Danny had joined them that he had seen land, and he was even more surprised to find that he recognised the place. He had only ever seen pictures of it, but it was so distinctive that there couldn't possibly be any mistaking it. For some reason that he never discovered, the Giant's Causeway on the coast of Northern Ireland, was a place of great significance for the merpeople.

The feel of land beneath his hands and feet brought all kinds of emotions into Danny's heart. He realised that he must have passed within a few miles of his father's home in Cork. Whether he would have risked visiting or not he couldn't decide, but he wished that he had known, all the same. And he also knew that he wasn't all that far away from Scotland and Fourth World.

The knowledge created a severe conflict in him. He longed to see Maggie and Tina and Oggy and the other animals in the strange community that had once been his home. But he was afraid of leaving the merpeople in case he couldn't find them again. The land would always be there, after all. He would always be able to find Fourth World if he decided to go back. But finding his tribe again might not be so easy.

They left the coast again well before dawn and continued to travel northwards. Inside a day, Danny understood why they had made the long journey from the warmer, more hospitable waters of the south. He had been aware for some time that the clan he was with was a small one, compared to the other groups they had encountered along the way. Off the north coast

of Ireland, they rejoined the rest of their kins-
folk, and Danny realised that his friends were
only part of the tribe, a party, perhaps, who had
been sent from their feeding grounds to follow
The Privateer and and rescue him. The others
had waited in the cold northern waters for their
return, and within hours of their arrival the
whole clan began to move southwards again,
back the way they had come.

Danny followed, his heart still heavy with
conflict. But they hadn't gone far when something happened that galvanised him into a
completely unexpected plan of action. Despite
his previous failures, a fourth child, another
member of the same unfortunate tribe of merpeople, was brought to him. And this time,
Danny suddenly knew what it was that he had
to do.

The mysterious illness was clearly outside the
experience of the merpeople, but Danny had
thought of someone else who might know what
to do. He took the child from its distraught
parents and, as they and the rest of his own
clan followed, he began to swim strongly back
towards the north.

4

One afternoon, as we were trudging along in our usual, ponderous line, Bernard suddenly came racing back across his own footprints and herded us like sheep into a huddle against the mountain wall. It wasn't until we had collared the dogs and calmed our pounding hearts that we heard the sound that had caused him to react so unexpectedly.

Somewhere in the distance, a helicopter was buzzing across the mountainside.

'It's probably the Chinese,' said Bernard. 'Patrolling the area.'

Loki tried to wriggle out of her collar, barking and choking. 'Huey-bird!' she coughed. 'Ak-ak-ak stations!'

'It must mean we're nearly there,' Bernard went on. 'And that we're going down. Those things can't operate much above twenty thousand feet, and I'd be willing to bet they don't take them anywhere near that high.'

'Nearly where?' said Colin.

'Civilization,' said Bernard. 'Just as well, too. We're nearly out of food.'

We had all noticed the dwindling supplies but

none of us had said anything, even to each other. It was a sign of how frightened we all were, and of how much we had surrendered our wills to Bernard's.

'Are we nearly in Tibet, then?' I asked.

'Tibet?' said Bernard. 'We've been in Tibet for ten days.'

The following morning, as we came through the neck of yet another snowy valley, Bernard called a halt. We had left the highest mountains behind and were now walking among a cluster of much smaller ones; a range of jutting crags or mini-peaks.

Bernard examined the maps as he waited for everyone to catch up and, when we were all gathered, he pointed to a col at the other side of the valley.

'Just over there,' he said.

We all whooped and stamped and cheered, even Sandy, and Loki ran in dizzying circles around us, frantic with excitement.

But the journey wasn't over yet. Not quite.

We crossed the valley, and by early afternoon we were climbing towards the nearest end of the col. We were almost at the top when Sandy gave a shout and pointed. At the other end of the snowy saddle, just below the opposite peak, was a dark spot in the snow. Bernard looked through the binoculars and handed them to me.

'It's a cave,' he said. 'Should we go and take a look?'

He didn't meet with much enthusiasm and, in the end, we agreed that Bernard and Colin would go and investigate the cave, taking a tent and one of the stoves in case they got overtaken by night. The rest of us would carry on, pitch camp somewhere on the other side of the col, and wait there until they caught up with us.

About two hours later, Sandy and I rounded the flank of the little peak beside it and saw, for the first time in two weeks, a grey-green valley stretching out below us. Its vast hill-sides were bleak and bare, but its folds and hollows sheltered tiny hamlets and groves of trees. After so long in a blue and white world, the sight of so much colour was a shock to our systems. I took off my snow-goggles and stared until Sandy diverted my attention.

'What do you think that is?' she said.

Just below the snowline, a mile or two away, was something that looked like a handful of sugar cubes tipped out of a bowl.

'Are they buildings?' said Sandy. 'Is it some kind of institution?'

'We could get there before dark and find out,' I said. 'But I suppose we'd better pitch camp and wait.'

We were just setting out to look for a likely spot when we heard a shout coming from behind us.

Bernard and Colin had arrived at the cave

mouth, only to be met with disappointment. It wasn't, in fact, a cave at all, but a shallow hollow which the snow had not managed to fill. It would have made a useful shelter for a man or a beast caught out in a storm, but there was nothing to suggest that it was, or ever had been, a haunt of the abominable snowman.

They started back straight away, deciding to take a short-cut across the lowest point of the col. Luckily, Bernard was lagging well behind, weighed down by the weight of all the gear. Even luckier was the fact that Roxy, uncharacteristically for him, was trotting along at his heels. Colin reached the top of the ridge well ahead of them both.

He too was gobsmacked by the view, and stood for some time in silent awe. Then he saw us, and that was when he shouted.

We waved back, and Colin shouted again and waved his arms, gesturing for us to wait for them. There was no way that he could have known that the ground he was standing on wasn't a true ridge at all. It was a cornice; a build-up of windblown snow, as unstable as a dried-out sandcastle. And Colin was already doing the worst thing he could possibly do.

He jumped and shouted one last time, and then the world erupted into chaos. There was a roar and a crash like a mighty wave breaking as the cornice collapsed, sending hundreds and thousands of tons of snow plunging on to the steep slope below. A moment later the air was filled with it, and we were standing in an ice cloud; the breath of the thundering avalanche.

Sandy sprang away from me and vanished into it. I made to follow but the powdery snow shifted under my feet, and I called urgently to Sandy to come back. A moment later, realising the danger for herself, she returned. For a long, long time we stayed where we were, stunned and helpless. Then, as the breeze began to blow gaps in the ice cloud, we got our first glimpse of the extent of what had happened. Where Colin had been, a huge, crescent-shaped chunk of the ridge had fallen away. Below, where the trail of the avalanche scarred the smooth slope, there seemed no chance at all of a small human being surviving.

PART EIGHT

1

When Bernard realised what had happened he dropped his pack and retraced his earlier steps to where they had first parted from ours. Despite the thin air he ran along our trail and appeared just as the ice cloud was finally dispersed by the wind.

As he came up to us he was gasping for breath, and I could see the pulse galloping dangerously in his throat.

'Where is he?' he gasped. 'Where's Colin?'

No one answered, but all our eyes rested on the jumbled trail of the avalanche. Hushy was already down there, braving the cold to try and find some trace of him. Before his blood froze he flew back and dived under my jacket. It felt as if someone had dropped a snowball in there.

Bernard looked down into the valley and pointed out the buildings we had observed earlier.

'Get there,' he shouted. 'Run! Fetch help!'

I didn't hang about, but someone had reacted even faster to Bernard's command. Already far below me on the slope, Loki was moving like a bat out of hell. I called after her as I ran, but I was wasting my breath.

Inside my jacket, Hushy was fluttering wildly, panicked by my desperation. Without pausing in my headlong descent, I let him out.

'Go after Loki,' I told him.

He shot off in pursuit and, slipping and falling and sliding and running again, I tried to catch up with them both. Never in all my life had I covered ground so fast.

The pile of sugar cubes was a monastery. Hundreds of monks, of all ages and back-grounds, lived and worked and prayed within its walls. The avalanche had been noticed, and several of the younger monks were still standing around the main gates, staring at the aftermath, discussing its causes and its portent.

They were good, hard-working students, well practised in meditation and control of the wandering mind. The words that they spoke were measured and calm. But when a black dog burst in through the main gates and hurtled straight into their midst, the composure of the youths deserted them. The gathering exploded like a firework and red-robed boys scattered in all directions.

Loki tried to run after them all at once, shouting 'Monstrous-catastrophe! Puffball kaboum!'

But in twenty seconds the courtyard was

empty, and every door that opened on to it had been firmly slammed and bolted.

The trail of the avalanche was still precarious with tons of snow ready to start sliding again but, despite the danger, the others had started the search. Roxy was tireless, tracking back and forth across the icy rubble, struggling through the deep, powdery pockets, using his nose like a metal detector. The others had to be more cautious. One of Sandy's bounds started a minor slip and she had to content herself with pussyfooting about like Bernard, calling softly all the time.

About a quarter of a mile from the monastery I misjudged a jump from a rock and felt something give in my ankle. I thought I would be able to ignore it and keep going, but when I tried to get up the pain was excruciating, and I found that I couldn't even limp.

But I had to go on. I just had to. Gritting my teeth against the pain, I hobbled and hopped and slid on my bum, determined to get help.

Inside its walls, Loki was racing around the streets and alleys and yards, still looking for someone to talk to. Hushy had joined her now and, finding that the temperature was tolerable at the lower altitude, had no need to return to me. Instead, he fluttered above the buildings, an aerial look-out for Loki.

But he didn't find anyone, either. The news of the rabid dog had spread quickly, and every monk in the place was safely shut in.

Or almost every monk. As Loki came out of an alleyway into a small, dark courtyard, she spotted a small robed figure, sitting cross-legged in the shadows.

She bounded over to him and licked his cold cheeks. 'Amass monkey-men,' she said. 'Up, up, heavenly-high! Dally-not!'

The monk, who was an old, old man, neither got up nor pushed Loki away. When Hushy flew down and joined them, he smiled at him happily.

'Please come, please come, please come,' said Hushy. 'One of our people, people, has been caught by an avalanche, avalanche. We need help, we need help, we need help.'

The old man chattered back in Tibetan and Hushy realised that he hadn't understood.

'Mumblespeak,' said Loki. 'Muddlebrain.'

'Wrong language,' Hushy explained.

Loki tried another form of communication. She dashed a few yards from the monk and looked back invitingly, hoping that he would follow. When he didn't, she bounced up to him and started to tug at his copious sleeve. Still he didn't get up. Instead, he put a gentle hand on Loki's head, and a very strange thing happened. All her nervous energy deserted her in an instant. She relaxed, sat down, and gazed into the old man's eyes.

And he found there what he hadn't heard in her voice or seen in her actions. He jumped up and moved with surprising energy from door to door, speaking softly but urgently, gathering support.

I was still making my painful way down the mountain path when Loki came charging back.

'Slow-bones,' she said, winding herself round my legs.

'Don't do that, Loki,' I said. 'I fell and hurt my ankle. That's why I've taken so long.'

I should have known better than to expect any sympathy from her. As she set off again up the steep track, I was sure that I heard her say, 'Dork!'

A few minutes later, a column of searchers came walking up the path. At the time, I had no idea that they were monks. Their robes were concealed beneath a variety of jackets and cloaks, and they were all strapping young men. They strode up the hill with impressive speed, and they still had enough breath left to chat with one another as they went.

When they saw me they all stopped and gathered round solicitously. One of them spoke good English, and he asked me if I was all right. I explained what had happened, and two of them stayed behind to help me the rest of the way to the monastery, while the others went on. As I watched them, I realised with a shock that each of them was carrying a torch or a lantern. None of them were lit, yet, but they soon would be. I hadn't noticed it before, but the night was drawing in fast.

2

The monks were very kind to me. I was given into the care of a middle-aged man called Lobsang, who not only spoke good English but happened to be some kind of doctor as well. He made a careful examination of my ankle and told me that it was sprained, not broken, and that the only cure for it was rest.

'You will have to stay here,' Lobsang said. 'Or get someone to carry you out.' He was strapping up my ankle as he spoke, with a bandage stitched together from several lengths of faded orange cloth. 'No such thing as a wheel in Tibet.'

'Really?' I said.

He smiled wistfully. 'Not near here. But there are plenty around Lhasa now, since the Chinese came. Before that, Tibet had no use for the wheel.'

'You mean no wheels at all? No carts or bicycles or trains?'

Lobsang shook his head. 'Only prayer-wheels,' he said.

It was dark outside now and growing colder by the minute. Lobsang must have seen the

187

concern on my face, but he didn't pull any punches.

'Not much hope for your friend. Very few survive an avalanche. The weight of the snow is too great.'

He didn't need to spell it out. If they hadn't rescued Colin by now, it was probably already too late. If the fall hadn't killed him, the cold soon would.

The searchers must have been well aware of that fact but they didn't give up. For hour after hour they trudged up and down in the rubble, until the torch batteries gave out and the lanterns had burned all their oil. Even then they continued to search, while the night grew colder and clearer and their fingers and toes became dangerously numb.

A sudden cry sent a wave of excitement through the party. Bernard and Sandy raced recklessly across the avalanche path to where the monks were converging on one of their companions. But he hadn't found Colin. He had started a serious slippage and had narrowly escaped being buried in it.

It seemed like a signal, not only to the superstitious monks, but to the others as well. Everyone had to agree that there was no point in prolonging the search. Everyone, that was, except Roxy.

Bernard called and called him, but he wouldn't come. While the others made their way to the monastery, he stayed above on the mountain-side, refusing to give up on Colin.

3

The monks did their best to comfort Bernard and, even though they were disconcerted by her appearance, Sandy. They were both so exhausted and traumatised that they hardly knew where they were. When they had warmed up and been persuaded to drink some butter tea, we were all introduced to one of the senior monks, who proposed that he and some of the others would carry out a ceremony for Colin, to help his soul make a successful passage into the next world. But Sandy was not allowed to attend. It wasn't, apparently, because she had frog genes and looked like a walking ghost, but because she was female, which seemed to cause the monks even more consternation. In some kind of solidarity, I stayed out with her in our personal quarters beside the bright log fire.

We hadn't much to say. Hushy sat on the stone mantel, soaking up the heat. Loki had been missing for a while and I wished that she was there where I could keep an eye on her. I dreaded to think what mischief she might be getting up to.

After a while, my friend Lobsang brought

food for us and a big kettle of hot tea. Our hearts were heavy but our famished bodies couldn't be denied, and we made short work of any tsampa that could be kept away from Hushy's ravenous beak. It would take us all a few more days, however, to develop a taste for the rancid butter tea.

When Loki finally appeared she had a friend with her. It was the old monk that had raised the alarm when she first arrived at the monastery. Lobsang introduced us all, and the old man, Tenpa, came to share the hearth with us. He had no English, so Lobsang stayed as well and acted as our interpreter.

After we had all exchanged our names and our ages and, for some obscure reason, our favourite colours, Tenpa began to say things that surprised us.

'Your dog and your little brown bird have human minds,' he said. 'This has never been seen in Tibet.'

Sandy and I exchanged glances. 'It's not very common in our country, either,' I told him.

Tenpa seemed to accept this without question, and turned his attention to Sandy. He gazed at her with clear, innocent eyes until she began to squirm with embarrassment. He apologised, and then said, 'You have the heart of a frog.'

Sandy and I were shocked into silence, and after a moment or two, Lobsang began to speak.

'You are lucky that Tenpa is here with us today,' he said. 'He is the only one of the monks that has the power . . .' He struggled for words. 'To see between worlds,' he went on. 'To see what cannot be seen.'

Tenpa, of course, understood none of this. As Lobsang spoke, his face had taken on an intense but unfocused expression, as though he was listening to some distant music.

'Isn't he always here?' said Sandy. 'Where does he go?'

'No one knows,' said Lobsang. 'Tenpa has mysterious habits. He spends a lot of time away from the monastery.'

As he was talking, Tenpa came out of his trance.

'Another dog,' he said, and Lobsang translated. 'A fox-dog with a human mind.'

I looked around, wondering if Roxy had slipped in without my noticing. But he hadn't.

'And a boy,' Tenpa went on. 'A boy with the blood of a fish.'

For an instant, my grip on reality slackened. He had never seen Roxy or Colin, and it was impossible that anyone could have told him.

'How do you know?' I said. 'Where are they?'

'On the mountain,' Lobsang translated. 'Where the avalanche fell.'

I was still too amazed to think straight, but Sandy was more on the ball.

'Alive?' she asked. 'Both of them alive?'

Lobsang passed on the question, and

192

returned Tenpa's confident reply. 'I cannot see the souls of those who go beyond. Only those who are still here.'

There wasn't one among the monks who sought to question Tenpa's vision. Within minutes, a new search party had gathered, dressed themselves against the cold and vanished into the night.

Lobsang and Sandy went with them, and Hushy and I were left alone with Tenpa. He turned his steady gaze upon me and it was my turn to squirm.

'Don't bother,' I said, even though I knew he couldn't understand me. 'You won't find any kind of animal heart in me.'

But I was surprised by my own feelings as I said it. I found that I was jealous of Sandy, and of Danny, even though he wasn't with us any more. I envied their amazing abilities, and felt myself to be inferior. It was boring being human, compared to them.

Tenpa grinned from ear to ear, and I had the uncomfortable sensation that he knew exactly what I was thinking. He pointed to me, then tapped his own chest and made an expansive gesture, as though we were holding a beach ball. I had no idea at all what he was trying to say.

4

Sandy, since she had already been clearly seen by the monks, made no attempts to hide her abilities. She bounded on ahead with Loki, leaving the rest of the group to gape after her in astonishment. The beam of her torch bounced up the mountain-side at what seemed to be an impossible speed and the others raced after it until, realising that they could never keep up, they slowed to a more sustainable pace.

High on the slope, Roxy saw the torches coming and shook his freezing body hard. His doggedness had paid off when, an hour or so after the others had abandoned the search, he picked up the faintest scent of Colin and found his nose protruding from the snow. Incredibly, though nothing else of the boy was visible, the nose was still working; still drawing breath. Roxy had ripped the boots from his front paws and, with infinite care, cleared the snow away from Colin's face.

It wasn't until then that he realised the extent of his dilemma. Colin was alive but unconscious; he clearly couldn't get up and walk away. But if Roxy went for help, how could he be sure

of finding him again? It had taken long enough
the first time. He could, he knew, leave his own
musky scent trail across the snow, but even that
seemed too risky. He mistrusted the mountains,
mistrusted the biting winds, mistrusted above
all the treacherous, shifting snows which might,
at any minute, start crashing around the place
again.

The cold was beginning to get into his bones.
For a few minutes, he yipped and barked at the
top of his voice, but he could tell by the speed
and direction of the wind that the sounds
wouldn't carry. He was left with only two
choices. Leave Colin and risk not finding him
again, or stay and hope that he would wake.

He stayed, and once again his loyalty and
determination were repaid. As soon as the first,
rapid torch-beam came near enough, he began
to bark again. Within minutes, Sandy and Loki
were at his side.

5

It was dead of night when Maggie was woken by a furious barking downstairs. As she reached for her bedside light, Oggy came rushing into her bedroom, saying 'Mother, Mother, Mother! Somebody's at the door.'

As she got up and put on her dressing gown, Maggie knew that something was wrong. She ought to have heard the dogs out on patrol before the ones in the house. Someone, somehow had silenced them. The first thought that sprang to her mind was the greatest and most constant of her fears. Sooner or later, one of the roaming armies was sure to discover Fourth World.

Tina was already out on the landing, and she followed Maggie down the stairs. Whoever had come was at the back door, not the front, which was strange in itself. The dogs were behaving oddly, growling and wagging their tails at the same time, as though they were getting mixed messages.

'Who's there?' Maggie called from inside the door.

'It's me, Mother. It's Danny.'

Maggie's heart leaped as she unbolted the door and pulled it open. But the sight that met her eyes made the blood stall in her veins. It was Danny, all right, but not the Danny she knew and loved. He was naked from head to foot, apart from some strands of weed which bound a primitive spear to his side. His uncut hair straggled around his face, and his skin was as pale as the full moon which hung, as though watching, above his shoulder. But worst of all, he was carrying something dreadful in his arms.

Maggie's first thoughts were terrifying. A story she had once read came into her mind, about a mother who wishes her dead son would return. Her wish comes true, but not as she had intended. The son's corpse rises from the grave, and arrives on her doorstep stinking of cold earth and decay.

Maggie stepped back and looked again at her son.

'Help me, Mother,' he said. 'Help her.'

6

Colin was already back in the monastery before anyone thought to inform the funeral party that he might not be needing their guidance into the next world after all. But Bernard's delight was tempered by concern when he saw him. He was still senseless, and his body temperature was a lot lower than ought to have been possible.

He was brought into our room and laid on a pile of thick rugs where Lobsang could examine him. After a few tense minutes he turned to us, looking puzzled.

'It's very strange,' he said. 'This boy is too cold to be alive. And yet he is alive. Even stranger than that, he has no sign of frostbite at all.'

As he spoke, Colin stirred and coughed and Bernard leapt to his side. His concern for Colin was obvious, and when I came to think about it I realised that they were unusually dependent upon each other, even for a father and son. I had never got much of a feeling for Colin as an individual – he was a lot younger than me and we didn't have much in common. It seemed to me that in some strange way he hadn't really developed his own personality yet, but existed as an extension of his father, thinking and acting in much the same way. I supposed that they must have developed a very deep understanding during the time they had spent together. Bernard was clearly frantic about his condition. I just wished that he had shown such concern for Danny.

Lobsang turned to Bernard and spoke gently. 'He has a swelling on his head. He must have hit it during the fall. But his pulse is strong. Very strong.'

'His fish pulse,' said Sandy, remembering Tenpa's words.

A strange expression came over Bernard's face, but he said nothing.

'We will let him warm up very slowly,' said Lobsang. 'And meanwhile I must look at your little red dog. He does, I'm afraid, have frostbite.'

He did, even on the paws that still had their boots on. He was suspicious of Lobsang and wouldn't let him touch him at first, but when Tenpa laid a hand on his back he went limp, and allowed them to do as they pleased. Lobsang went away and fetched a herbal paste, which he spread on all the paws before bandaging them up in more of the peach-coloured cloth.

By the time the operation was over, Colin was showing more signs of returning life. Over the next hour his temperature came up to normal and soon after that he opened his eyes and asked where he was.

The sun was already up before Lobsang finally announced that he was sure Colin was out of danger. We were all desperately tired and wanted to get some sleep, but Tenpa and Lobsang refused to let us rest until we had given them some answers, and we had to admit that, after all they'd done for us, they deserved them.

So, as the other monks chanted their morning prayers in the compound nearby, we filled our new friends in on the story of Fourth World and the work that had been done there. As time went on, their eyes grew larger.

'You mean the animals speak?' said Lobsang.

'Didn't Tenpa tell you?' I said.

'Tenpa says many things that have an unusual interpretation. I didn't realise he meant it literally.' He glanced at Tenpa, who grinned delightedly.

'He did indeed,' said Roxy.

Lobsang stared at him for a long, long time, then said, 'I cannot believe it.'

He found it even more difficult to grasp the concept behind Sandy and Colin's modified genes.

'You mean your father was a frog?' he asked Sandy.

'My father is Bernard!' she said.

'Your mother, then?'

'No. no. It doesn't work like that. The genetic

material is introduced into the egg at the fertilization stage.'

This didn't square at all with what Lobsang knew about the fertilization stage, and he was clearly finding it very difficult to translate what he was hearing for the benefit of Tenpa. But everyone was too tired to go into the details, and Bernard promised to give him a better explanation another time.

We started to get ourselves ready for bed, but Lobsang had one more question. 'But what about this one? He doesn't look like a fish.'

I thought Colin was asleep, but he had clearly been listening.

'I was a failure,' he said. 'I was supposed to have gills so I could breath underwater, but it didn't work.'

'Oh yes,' said Bernard. 'I meant to tell you what I worked out about you last night.'

'What?' said Colin.

'Maggie and I never understood what went wrong with that experiment,' said Bernard. 'Not only did the gills not appear, but you didn't seem to have any fishy attributes at all.'

'He's a funny colour,' said Sandy.

'That's true. But that was all.'

'Go on,' said Colin. 'Keep talking.'

'Well,' said Bernard. 'We obviously made a mistake, and isolated the wrong part of the salmon DNA. But that mistake saved your life out there in the snow.'

'How?' said everyone at once.

'You must have got the gene that scientists have known about for years. It's even been put into plant species to protect them against frost. Strawberries and such.'

'So that's why his blood didn't freeze?' I said. 'No frostbite.'

'Exactly,' said Bernard. 'Colin didn't get gills. He got the anti-freeze gene instead.'

7

It took Maggie and Tina quite some time to get over the shock of Danny's arrival. Now that he was back in the familiar surroundings of Fourth World, he could understand how the merchild must appear to them. Underwater, the sea people were natural and graceful, perfectly adapted to their environment, even beautiful. But in the bright light of Maggie's kitchen, the child looked grotesque. Her skin was coarse and blotchy. Her remaining hair was like tangled, greeny-black twine. And the thick whiskers that grew from her face were like ghastly, overgrown warts. Worst of all, her large, pale eyes were wide and staring. Danny hadn't realised it until then, but on the last leg, up through the glen, he had lost her.

Now he laid her out on the kitchen table and arranged her slack limbs. Maggie and Tina could hardly bear to look at her, but they could hardly resist doing so, either, and while Danny filled them in on the merpeople's plight, they gradually became accustomed to the sight.

'So you have to help them, you see?' he said, accepting Maggie's dressing gown and putting it on. 'You have to find out what killed her and tell us how to cure the others.'

Maggie hugged her son tight, and he hugged her back.

'I'm so glad to see you, Danny,' she said. 'I thought you were dead.'

Tina hugged Danny as well. He smelled of the sea. 'You're not going back to them, are you?' she said. 'You're staying here with us in Fourth World?'

Danny looked distressed and didn't answer. He turned to his mother instead. 'Can you help them?'

Maggie shook her head helplessly. 'I don't know, Danny. But I'll try.'

8

We stayed in the monastery for more than two weeks, and the monks were wonderfully kind and hospitable. Lobsang kept an eye on my ankle and set a programme of exercise for me, to keep me from seizing up completely while my sprain healed. In the evenings we often discussed religion and philosophy, and because Lobsang never made any attempts to convert me I allowed myself to become quite interested in Buddhism and Tibetan culture. I even took a few lessons in meditation, and Loki and I learnt to chant 'Om mane padme hum,' and still our restless minds. Well, a bit, anyway.

Loki and Roxy and Hushy became very fond of Tenpa and spent a good deal of time with him between his mysterious absences. He had a pattern; three or four days in the monastery and three or four days away. Lobsang said it had been the same way for years. He did not explain where he went, and no one ever asked him. It was understood by everyone in the community that someone with powers like his was entitled to do as he pleased.

I enjoyed his company as well, even when

there was no one around to translate for us. He emanated peace and, despite his astonishing abilities, seemed to be completely devoid of any kind of conceit. Sometimes, when I found myself alone in the room, I would sit quietly and try to send my mind off searching as he did. But it never worked for me.

Colin had a headache for twenty-four hours after his argument with the mountain, but otherwise he was fine. For a day or two Bernard was subdued, and it occurred to me that the shock of Colin's accident might have sobered him up a bit, and driven his yeti fantasies out of his mind. But if it was true, it didn't last long. He made enquiries among the monks, several of whom claimed to have seen the yeti, and on their advice he set off on new expeditions, of two or three days at a time, in search of his elusive quarry. Colin went with him and so did Sandy, although I got the distinct impression that she did it as much to spite him as to enjoy herself. Loki was too attached to me to leave and Roxy, like me, was laid up for a while.

One evening, when the others were away on one of their trips, I was sitting on my own beside the fire, regretting that I hadn't gone with them. My ankle was pretty much mended, and I was bored with lounging around doing nothing, day after day. So I was pleased when Lobsang and Tenpa came to visit me. At least, I was until I discovered what they wanted to talk about.

It was a difficult conversation for all concerned. Tenpa wanted to know how Sandy and Colin and the animals had originated, and between my inability to explain things clearly and Lobsang's laborious translation attempts, I had the distinct impression that Tenpa wasn't learning much. I told them all I could about genetic engineering and cloning, but I could tell that it wasn't making much sense to Tenpa. He asked me why we were looking for the yeti, and I burbled on a bit about the missing link and its unknown origins. None of my attempts satisfied him, though. 'Because it's there, I suppose,' I said at last. 'Like Everest. Or at least, because it might be.'

Both of them were totally confused by that, and it brought the conversation to an end. Tenpa went away, clearly uneasy, and Lobsang stayed for a while, smiling at me as though he was humouring a madman.

But it must have had some effect. Tenpa left the monastery the next day and when he came back a few days later he paid another visit, along with Lobsang, to our room. The others had recently returned from their third fruitless expedition, so we were all gathered around the fire, a bit gloomy and bored with each other.

Tenpa wasted no time. Lobsang translated what he said.

'You will come with me tomorrow. Be ready at first light.'

'Come where?' we all asked. But he had already turned on his heel and gone.

207

9

When we presented ourselves to him in the morning he shook his head and pointed to the animals.

'One of us will have to stay behind, then,' said Bernard. I had already turned away, masking my disappointment, when Bernard called me back. 'Not you, Christie. You need to give that ankle a spin.'

He looked at Sandy, who was back in her veil for the mystery tour, just in case. Clearly he expected her to volunteer in my place. She didn't. She stood firm.

'You choose, Dad,' she said.

Bernard clenched his teeth and turned his face up to the skies in irritation. But the necessity for him to choose between his children was removed by Tenpa, who took Sandy's arm and led her towards him.

'This girl must come,' said Lobsang.

Bernard was slightly taken aback. 'Oh, all right then,' he said. 'Do you mind, Col?'

Colin did, clearly, though he appeared to be more anxious than angry. The bond between him and his father was so strong.

'You'll be fine with the monks,' Bernard went on. 'I'm sure we won't be away for long.'

Sandy was pleased, but if she had expected it to improve her standing with Bernard, she was heading for more disappointment. He ignored her quite pointedly, and before long she dropped to the rear of the little column and plodded along dejectedly, as hurt as if he had insisted she stay behind. But as time went by Bernard forgot about it all and began to grow manic with excitement.

'Where do you think he's taking us?' he asked me, over and over again.

'Why don't you ask him?' I finally suggested.

'No,' he said. 'No. I couldn't do that.'

I dropped back to walk with Sandy.

We were crossing a broad stretch of frozen grassland. Beneath the sparse growth, the soil was cold and hard. There was no one around.

Sandy threw back her veil. 'Do you believe me now?'

'Believe what?' I said.

'That he hates me?'

I wished I could say no. But I couldn't.

10

Maggie carried out an amateur post-mortem on the merchild in the operating theatre in the underground lab complex. Now that she had recovered from the shock her revulsion had been replaced by an intense scientific curiosity. As she worked, she reflected on the possibility that Bernard's ideas might not be so hare-brained after all. If merpeople existed, maybe yetis did as well.

Maggie took her time over the examination, and took care to keep the strange creature as intact as was possible. It wasn't long before she began to find evidence of the disease that had killed her. There were pockets of blood at various places beneath the skin. The lungs were full of discoloured fluid, suggesting that pneumonia was one of the causes of death. But it was clearly a secondary, not a primary cause. Because every organ in the child's body seemed to have been damaged. The liver and kidneys were pocked with lesions, and there were weaknesses in all the major blood vessels. The brain, like the lungs, was full of fluid.

Maggie wished she knew more. The disease

had clearly overwhelmed the whole system, but that didn't help Maggie to understand what it was. She took samples from various parts of the body, sealed them in flasks and put them in the fridge. Then she stitched up the little corpse, carried it back to the house, and made space for it in the smaller of the two freezers in the scullery. If Bernard ever came home, she wanted him to see it.

11

I had expected that our journey would take us up into the snows, but it didn't; at least, not to begin with. Tenpa led the way down the hill, through the local village and along a series of narrow paths that meandered around the mountain-side well below the snowline. For a few miles we walked through sparse forest and across scree-clad slopes, the only signs of life being the lightly-worn paths that we were following. Cold, clear streams ran down from the heights, and once we crossed a half mile of slippery, stone-strewn ice that Lobsang told us was the tongue of a glacier.

Soon after that, we entered an area of cultivated land, the irrigated crops bursting out in electric greens, surprising our complacent sight. As we approached the settlement in the middle of the farmland, Tenpa indicated that the rest of us should follow at a distance, and allow him to pass through the village alone. We did as he asked, shadowing him at a hundred yards, but keeping him in sight throughout.

The reaction of the villagers to Tenpa was remarkable. Everyone in the vicinity came out on to the street to bow to him, or to touch his feet, or merely to smile and receive the blessing of his raised hand. Some of them gave him gifts, which we later learned were fistfuls of rice, an egg, a withered apple, a few sticks of firewood. To us it didn't seem much, but to the villagers, barely subsisting on the cold soil, the gifts represented a great generosity.

We, however, met with an entirely different kind of reaction. Whereas most Nepalis were quite accustomed to seeing foreigners trekking past their homes, these Tibetans clearly weren't. The more courageous stared at us wide-eyed as we passed, and called out questions that Lobsang answered politely. The others slipped back inside their doorways and watched nervously from the shadows.

We passed through several more villages during the day and at each one the same ritual was observed. We hung back and Tenpa went ahead, collecting gifts and bestowing blessings. Before the day was out he had collected a bagful of food and, to our amusement, a pair of spritely young goats, who frisked on leads at his heels like overgrown pups.

As dusk began to fall, Tenpa led us away from the well-kept villages and back towards the snowline. We walked on into the night, our way illuminated by the blue light reflecting from the snow, until we came to a stone cabin which stood alone in the pale wilderness; a shelter,

Lobsang told us, for herders crossing the pass in the summer months.

Tenpa lit a fire and cooked a simple meal from the villagers' gifts, singing to himself all the while. I had the impression that he had made this journey many times before and, although he was aware of our graceless presence, he preferred to ignore it most of the time.

After we had eaten and settled ourselves and the goats on the cleanest parts of the floor, Bernard summoned the courage to ask the question that was on everybody's mind.

'Where are we going?'

Lobsang translated the question and, though he seemed to be perturbed by it, the answer.

'You have said that you want to see the yeti, yes?'

PART NINE

1

While Maggie was reading up everything she could find about viruses and infections, Tina took advantage of Danny's presence to get some repair work done on the dam. It had sprung a leak near the bottom, and although it wasn't too serious yet, if it wasn't fixed soon it would gradually undermine the whole structure and leave Fourth World without hydroelectric power.

Danny was happy to oblige. Tina humped materials up from the buildings and he carried out the underwater repairs. While he was there, he found a few other weak spots as well, and in the end he spent two whole days on the job.

But Maggie was getting no closer to a solution. Although there were a number of viruses that could have produced some of the symptoms, there were none that accounted for them all. And when she put a sample of tissue into the electron microscope, looking for evidence of virus activity in the cells, she found a further symptom to add to the list. There was substantial chromosomal damage as well.

That night, she was woken by the solution knocking on the door of her dreams. As she opened her eyes, she was already certain that the word circulating in her mind was the right one. What surprised her was that she hadn't thought of it earlier. It was, after all, something which came into every scientist's education.

The noise of Maggie banging around in the scullery woke Danny and Tina, and they went downstairs to see what was happening. They found her working feverishly, loading the contents of the smaller freezer into empty grain bags and throwing them outside.

'Where's the merchild?' said Danny.

'Outside too,' said Maggie. 'Stay away from her. And don't let the dogs out, either.'

'What's happened?' said Tina. 'What are you doing?'

Maggie threw out the last of their carefully saved food and said, 'Help me with this, will you?'

The three of them lugged the heavy freezer outside and across the yard to the furthest of the outhouses, which had once been a stable for Tony's mother. There was no electricity in there, and Maggie ran a long cable from the feed shed to plug in the freezer. Then she ordered Danny and Tina back to the house and they watched through the windows while she retrieved the plastic-wrapped corpse and carried it to the stable.

When she came back she went upstairs and

washed herself from head to foot before she joined the others in the kitchen.

'What on earth was that all about?' said Tina.

'I'm almost certain I know what killed her,' said Maggie. 'Oh, Danny. It isn't good news.'

'Why?' said Danny. 'What is it?'

'Radiation sickness,' said Maggie. 'Somewhere out there in the sea there is a very, very bad leak.'

Danny would have left there and then to warn his friends of the danger, but Maggie wouldn't hear of it.

'You've been too close to it already,' she said, 'caring for those children. You may be sick yourself. You can't risk exposing yourself to any more contamination.'

Danny absorbed the information and saw the deep concern in his mother's face.

'At least I should take her back to them,' he said. 'They didn't want me to bring her ashore at all. They're afraid of being discovered.'

But Maggie wasn't going to be shifted. 'I don't want you touching her again. No one is to go anywhere near that freezer. If I'm right about her, we've all had a dose of radiation, and for the moment we have to stay put and keep an eye on each other.'

2

We were up before dawn in the morning, and as we ate a rapid breakfast outside the hut, an enormous bird of prey drifted across the valley beneath us.

'Lammergeier,' said Bernard.

'Most auspicious omen,' said Lobsang. 'Today will bring you much peace of mind.'

'That'll be the day,' said Sandy.

I had to admit that I couldn't see it, either. Whatever else the day might have in store for us, peace of mind seemed just about the most unlikely. Tenpa was already getting ready to set off, and if I had three guesses about where we were going, all of them would be up. If we didn't meet the yeti, Bernard would probably strangle us all before the day was out. And if we did . . .

I had the distinct impression as the day wore on that Tenpa, despite his advanced years, would have travelled a lot faster without us. He strode out ahead, as light-footed as the young goats who still trailed, a little less enthusiastically now, at his heels. The rarefied air seemed to suit him; he was a man in his element. For all our acclimatisation the rest of us, Lobsang included, were not.

We walked without a break for the whole of the morning and on into the afternoon. Sandy and Lobsang and I adopted a regular, shuffling rhythm to cope with the pace, but Bernard proceeded in fits and starts, taking regular pauses to scan the landscape. I wished he wouldn't. Tenpa had forbidden him to bring either maps or camera, and it seemed to me that he was breaking faith by taking such care to imprint the surroundings upon his memory. It added evidence to Sandy's assertion that he was untrustworthy. In spite of all I had already seen, I didn't want to believe that. Thoughtless I could accept; even careless. But I couldn't entertain the possibility, no matter how obvious it was becoming, that Bernard was merely unscrupulous. If he was, then nothing made sense. Not Fourth World, not the hunt for the yeti, not Danny's death.

It was a long time since I had thought about that. My knees went weak and I sat down in the snow. Lobsang called ahead to Tenpa, who nimbly retraced his steps to join us.

'Time for a halt,' said Lobsang. 'Time to take lunch.'

3

The sun vanished behind the high peaks long before the light left the sky. By now, Tenpa's pace had been slowed to something that matched the rest of us, mainly owing to the reluctance of the two young goats to follow him any further. They were tired and cold and hungry; the jaunt was turning into a nightmare. They bleated a lot and resisted their lead-ropes, but Tenpa never lost patience with them. He spoke softly to them, sang them little songs, tempted and teased and cajoled them into going along, always just a little bit further. But as the sun dropped lower, staining the snowscape pink, their resistance turned to obstinacy; they struggled desperately against their ropes, and Tenpa began to have serious difficulty holding them.

I had learned enough about animals by then to realise that this behaviour wasn't just an escalation of the ongoing protest. Something was scaring them. Some sense of theirs, far keener than mine, had warned them of a danger ahead. I had a feeling that we were approaching our destination.

Bernard helped Tenpa with the frantic creatures as he turned to his left and began to clamber up a steep incline, slippy with fresh snow, towards a cluster of huge, dark crags that broke through the whiteness above us. My heart felt as though it couldn't pump another ounce of blood through my veins. It might have been the effort of the climb, but I suspected that I had been infected by the unhinged terror of the goats, and I was inclined to sympathise with their reading of the situation. Whatever was up there, lurking among those crags, could stay there as far as I was concerned. I had no desire whatsoever to try and winkle it out.

I think Lobsang shared my views. In any event, he slackened his pace and brought up the rear with me. Before long, the others had vanished from sight around a steep spur of rock, and reluctantly, a step at a time, we followed. When we reached the spur there was no sign of them, but their tracks led clearly around the edge of the rock and into the mouth of an overhung cave. It was black as night in there and we hesitated. There was a strong, animal smell. The goats, if they were still alive, were silent.

A candle flickered. No one spoke, but the message of the candle, held quite still in the inner darkness, was clear. We were to go in.

4

They were all waiting for us, their faces pale and tense in the shadows. The goats were cowering against the wall, tethered to something beyond the reach of the light. There was a religious hush in the cave, far more reverent than any I had encountered in the monastery. As we stood there, peering forward into the dark interior, Tenpa uttered a long, low call.

It was answered from within by an echoing reply that made my hackles rise. Sandy edged closer to me. Tenpa, holding the candle, moved forward. The rest of us, even Bernard, held back.

The call came again from within. It set off every alarm in my system, and I had to struggle hard against the impulse to bolt. Sandy turned to me, and though I could barely see her in the retreating candlelight, I had a sense that she was moved by what she heard in a different, more complex way. The candle vanished around a turn in the cave wall. There was still a faint blue glow entering from the outside, and I had an urgent desire to move towards it. But Sandy moved forward, drawn by something stronger than curiosity, and some sense of fellowship compelled me to accompany her.

As we turned the bend in the rock wall, we could see Tenpa's outline, silhouetted by the candle. There appeared to be nothing but blank rock ahead of him, but as we caught up with him he shone the light upon a waist-high fault in the stone, then ducked down and crawled through it.

Without the slightest hesitation, Sandy followed. I lingered for a moment, aware of Bernard and Lobsang breathing in the gloom behind me. I knew that if I stopped to think about it I would never go in. I braced myself and ducked into the low channel.

I could see the candlelight immediately. The crawl distance was minimal; within a few feet the roof level rose again, and I was able to stand up beside Sandy. She didn't notice me, though, any more than I noticed Bernard and Lobsang as they squeezed through behind me. Because we found ourselves looking at the legend of the Himalayas; so often sought, never found. Tenpa had led us to the yeti.

5

What did I see? That time in the cave still haunts me when I try to recapture it. Everything had a surreal, dreamlike quality, like the time the bird, Darling, first spoke to me back in Ireland. What was happening defied the safe mental structures we work so tirelessly to erect. It couldn't be happening, but it was.

Was she an ape? If an ape is a humanoid creature with a hairy body, then I suppose she was. Her coat was long; in the soft light it gave off bright, gingery glints. But I still couldn't think of her as an ape. She was more than that. Much more. Her eyes were wide, with huge black pupils, evolved for the night and not for the day. Her frame was slender, but gave the impression that it was packed with dangerous power. She wasn't threatening, exactly, but she was a powerful presence; a myth standing upon the face of the earth; almost a god. I was fascinated and terrified at the same time. Like a mouse, I remember thinking. A mouse mesmerised by a cat. We were all like mice, huddling in the entry-way. No one spoke. No one moved. The silence was colossal.

The yeti's eyes moved over us and, as we waited to see what would happen next, it became clear to me that she was every bit as much unnerved by us as we were by her. Of course she was. There had never been expeditions sent to find and capture us. We hadn't had to spend our entire lives in hiding. By bringing us here, Tenpa had exposed the yeti to her greatest enemy. For the first time I took my eyes from her and glanced at Bernard. I hoped that Tenpa hadn't been mistaken in his trust.

I don't remember how long the silence went on, but I do remember that it became more comfortable. The yeti didn't seem to mind at all that we stared at her. She stared back, clearly as fascinated by us as we were by her. I wondered if she had ever seen a human being other than Tenpa. I wondered how he had come to befriend her. And then I had a sudden insight. She possessed the missing link gene. I had no doubts whatsoever about it. I could see it written in her eyes and in her manner. Even though she was anxious, she knew who we were. She had been expecting us.

How do you introduce yourself to a yeti? I wouldn't have had a clue, but it seemed to be no problem to Tenpa. He gave his heavily accented versions of our names in turn; 'Barnowl, Calee-stie, Someday.'

If the yeti had a name, it was something that

neither Tenpa nor Lobsang could translate. Her brown gaze held us each in turn, but it was upon Sandy that it rested for longest. I had the feeling that there was some invisible connection between them, a recognition that, for Sandy, had been evident when she first heard the haunting call.

Now that everyone was relaxing a bit, I was able to observe the yeti more closely. The backs of her hands were covered in hair, but her palms were bare, and looked as soft and sensitive as my own. She had an opposing thumb, like humans do, and it made me wonder if her race had ever developed tools. I glanced around but there were none to be seen. The place was clean and bare; the lair of a simple beast. Except that she was not a simple beast; I was certain of that.

I already had a hundred questions I wanted to ask Tenpa, but the yeti pre-empted me. The sounds she made this time were very different. Her voice was clear, full of round vowels and soft sibilance, like the music of the wind in the trees. Tenpa passed on her message to Lobsang, who translated for us.

'She is pleased that you have come. Tenpa has told her you can make . . .' He was lost for the right word, and gestured towards Sandy as an illustration of what he was trying to say. The yeti's gaze lingered upon her again.

'He told her? She speaks? She has a language?' Bernard could barely contain his excitement.

Tenpa nodded. 'Yeti language very beautiful. Very simple.'

'I knew it!' He turned towards Sandy and me. 'What did I tell you?'

Neither of us reacted. I'm sure that Sandy, like me, already knew. But Bernard's mood was triumphal. It made me uneasy. He turned back to address Tenpa again. 'How many of them are there? Do they have a community? Do they live in families?'

Tenpa shook his head when Lobsang translated for him. When he spoke his voice was quiet and subdued, and Lobsang answered us in the same tone. 'There are no more families. No communities. That is why he has brought you here. This yeti is the last of them all. She has asked if you can make her a mate.'

6

'A mate?' said Bernard.

'How can she be so sure,' I said, 'that she's the last one? I mean, these mountains are so big . . .'

Lobsang passed the question on. 'Yeti knows,' he said. 'Yeti has travelled the whole range. Besides, Tenpa also knows. In a different way.'

Tenpa was watching Bernard, still waiting for his response to the yeti's request. But Bernard seemed crestfallen. 'I wish we could help her,' he said. 'But we don't have that kind of technology yet. To make a male clone from a female model.'

Lobsang stared at Bernard for a minute or two, clearly wondering how to translate this technospeak into Tibetan. When he did make a stab at it, he seemed to have reduced it to the bare essentials. Tenpa, in turn, reduced it again in translation to the yeti.

'We could keep some of your genes . . .your bloodline . . .alive, though,' Bernard said. 'By introducing them into a human being. There would be a child who was part human, part yeti. Like Sandy here. She has frog genes.'

When the translation got back to her, the yeti looked long and hard at Sandy before she replied.

'She says she would not wish for that. She says the half-human child is as lonely as she is.'

7

Sandy said nothing, but her feelings infected every one of us there beneath the mountain. No one looked at her. No one moved. Our freezing breath made smoky plumes in the candlelight.

Eventually Bernard cleared his throat. 'I have a friend who has cloned sheep,' he said. 'If she would be willing, we can try and make a copy of her.'

'Here? Now?'

Bernard shook his head, and explained what he could of the process. 'Perhaps it wouldn't help you, here and now. But it would mean that your species would not die out. It's like another way for you to have a child. If we succeeded in cloning you, we could keep yetis on earth, perhaps for ever.'

The yeti asked what the process would entail. She seemed particularly concerned about where the cloning would take place, and where the newborn yeti would spend its life. Bernard told the truth. Assuming we could make it work, which wasn't guaranteed, she might never see the child. It would have to be born at Fourth World. The chances, after that, of getting it back to the Himalayas would be slim. But if it was important to her, we would try, of course.

The yeti took her time to absorb the new information, scrutinising each of us with her warm, brown gaze. Eventually, through the two translators, she gave us her answer.

'My people can never live happily among yours. If we could have, do you think we would have chosen to live up here, in the coldest place on the earth?'

'But that must have happened a long time ago,' I said. 'Perhaps things are different now. Perhaps people have changed.'

When my words had been filtered back to her, the yeti looked closely at me, and I had the uncomfortable feeling that she was reaching into my deepest thoughts; as though she could see there whether people had changed or not. I tried to hold her gaze; to show her what was good and trustworthy in me, but I couldn't withstand her scrutiny. I looked away.

Into the silence that followed, the yeti began to tell a story. She spoke in long, susurrating passages, and although her words had to pass into two more languages before they reached us, I was left with the strangest sensation; that somehow I had been able to understand her; that her story had passed straight from her mind into my own. I could see the details. I think we all could. The story was as much an imaginative process as a narrative.

'It can never be,' she said. 'My people do not have long lives, but they have long memories. Very long.'

She turned her melancholy gaze on to Sandy, but her eyes lost focus as she looked beyond her, into a time that human memory had long since lost. As her tale began to unwind, the stream of words flowed smoothly, taken up by Tenpa and Lobsang, crossing the boundaries of three languages as freely as a wild mountain stream.

'In the beginning, there were no human beings; only the yeti and the beasts which did not talk. We ranged far and wide across the earth, and the forests were ours, and the hills and the plains and the shores.

'But then the world began to change. Slowly, very slowly, the sea level rose. Our people took to the higher ground, where the forests were still thick and green and provided for all our needs.'

As the story progressed we began to unwind. Bernard edged closer to the yeti and sat down on his pack. Sandy and I hunkered down on our heels, our backs against the rough, cold walls.

'As time went on the high places became islands in a huge sea. Our populations became isolated from each other. Some of them were swallowed by the flood waters. Some ran out of food and starved. And some, my long-distant ancestors, were driven still higher, into the mountain territories. There was no snow then, but conditions were harsh. It was at that time, we are told, that we first began to kill the other beasts in order to feed ourselves. It was necessary in order to survive.'

Bernard was fiddling with something, quietly and, I thought, surreptitiously. The candle gave out so little light that it was difficult to see what he was doing, but I saw something in his hand that looked to me like a plastic film container. I glanced at Sandy. She was looking at him, too. I couldn't understand what he was doing. He had told everyone he didn't have a camera with him. Surely he hadn't lied?

'Slowly, very slowly, the flood waters dropped away again. Slowly, very slowly, the land began to heal from the sea's invasion, and grow green again. Slowly, very slowly, my people began to return to the valleys and plains of their ancestors. But there was a new breed of creature on the earth.'

The yeti eyed each of us in turn, and we were left in no doubt about what the new breed of creature looked like.

'That new creature did not understand our language. It spread across the land, making shelters, then villages. It gathered the other creatures that were the yeti's food and kept them for itself; it would not share. The yeti was not welcome in its own land.'

There was a soft pop as Bernard got the top off the film box. He looked embarrassed and lowered his head to his knees. It wasn't easy to see but I could just make out the fingers of his left hand, which seemed to be feeling around on the ground. He must have dropped something, but I couldn't see what.

'We retreated again, back to our old hunting grounds, and stayed in the mountains where we were safe from persecution. But your people kept on multiplying; they pushed their villages and farms further and further into our land until we had nowhere to go except where they could not survive. Up here, in the snow.'

Bernard stopped fiddling and returned the film container to his pocket. Sandy shot me a glance full of significance, but I was too absorbed by the yeti's story to pick up on her meaning.

'We lived in the only way we could. To begin with there were wild animals here, sharing the freezing wastes with us. But even they began to die out, and we were reduced to raiding the farmers in order to survive. Of course, we could not go on for ever like that. Our numbers fell. We could not replace our dead with young. And now . . .' The yeti touched her chest. 'And now there is only me. When I die, there will be no more yetis.'

8

It took a long time for the magnitude of what we had heard to sink in. The tiny candle trembled in the silence, and I was aware of the night awaiting us outside. My mind was still inhabiting that limbo place where parallel versions of reality existed in conflict with each other. I couldn't grasp the significance of the yeti's words, but I found myself remembering what Bernard had said about the Olduvai Gorge, where human and prehuman remains had been discovered. Could it all be true? Could any race have a memory that stretched back that far?

Why not? If the story had been passed on faithfully from generation to generation?

Bernard was the first to speak. He made another attempt to persuade the yeti to permit herself to be cloned. He said that she owed it to her ancestors to allow the race to continue, in any way possible. Since she would be unlikely to see the results of a cloning programme, she had no need to concern herself with the feelings of the individual that might result.

But she would not change her mind. She could not, she told us, inflict her own loneliness on another member of her species, no matter how, or where it might come into being. I could see that she was right, but I could understand Bernard's point as well. There was something so sad, so terribly final about the extinction of a species, and particularly one as fine and as advanced as the yeti. I was surprised, in fact, by how quickly and quietly he conceded the argument.

The emotional pressure was too much for Sandy. She stood up, and I caught the gleam of streaming tears as she turned towards the entrance and ducked into it. Bernard sighed deeply, and followed her out.

Not knowing what else to do, I made to follow. But a strange thing happened. As I rose to my feet the yeti began talking to Tenpa, and he gestured to me to stay where I was. I could hear distraught voices from the outer part of the cave. Bernard and Sandy were arguing again.

Inside, the yeti and Tenpa were still talking. They kept glancing in my direction, and after a while it became clear to me that, for some reason or other, their discussion was revolving around me. I began to feel uneasy and made for the exit again; but again Tenpa waved his hand and Lobsang smiled reassuringly.

'Please wait,' he said.

Outside, the argument was escalating and the goats had begun to add their opinions. The conversation within took on an air of urgency and then, abruptly, came to an end. At the same moment, Bernard and Sandy went quiet as well.

The only sound was a single, mournful cry from one of the goats. The yeti gave me a long, searching look, then seemed to come to a decision. She reached behind her, picked something up and handed it to me.

I thought it glowed briefly as she passed it over, but it must have been a trick of the shadows. What I held in my hand appeared to be a highly polished stone, a flattened black oval. It shone in the shifting light, but it didn't glow.

'It has been with the yeti since the beginning of time,' said Lobsang, translating for Tenpa. 'Now the yeti is gone. You must take care of it.'

I bent to examine it more closely, through the cloud of my frosted breath. I could only imagine that it was a tool of some kind. An axe head perhaps; a very finely-crafted one. But why should it be so significant to the yeti people?

I wasn't sure I liked the responsibility. 'Shouldn't you give it to Bernard?' I said. 'Or the monks?'

There was a scuffling at the entrance. Sandy and Bernard were on their way back. The yeti stepped smoothly forward, grabbed my hand, closed my gloved fingers over the stone and guided it rapidly into concealment, beneath the hem of my jacket.

It was all the only answer I ever got to my question, but it couldn't have been clearer.

9

My mind was tripping over itself with questions, but I didn't get the opportunity to ask them. Tenpa turned Bernard back immediately and, politely but firmly, he ushered Lobsang and I out after him.

When the goats saw Tenpa coming out, they launched into an outpouring of desperate bleats, imploring him to untie them and let them go home. It was hard to pass them by, knowing the fate that awaited them.

Sandy was heartbroken when she wasn't allowed to go back in. 'Say goodbye to her for me,' she said to Tenpa. 'Tell her she isn't alone. I'll never forget her.'

Sandy's tears were threatening to deprive Tenpa of his composure. He nodded helplessly and I had the feeling that, although he couldn't have understood a word that she said, he knew exactly what was in her mind. Bernard was seized by an agony of frustration. His face seemed to reflect her distress, almost as though he were feeling it along with her. I thought that the moment had come and some kind of reconciliation must surely take place. But Bernard's expression changed.

'For God's sake, Sandy,' he said. 'Pull yourself together.'

In the snowlight our tracks were quite clear, and Tenpa set out immediately to return along them. I dropped behind, and succeeded in stuffing the yeti's stone into the waistband of my trousers. Behind us, the goats called frantically. I tried to close my heart against their distress and hurried to catch up with Sandy. But she was distressed as well.

Although she had stopped crying, the spilled tears still lay on her face, frozen solid like tiny glaciers on her skin. We'd had such a short time with the yeti. Just a blink and it was over.

'That wasn't half long enough,' I said to Sandy.

I thought she was feeling the same way, but there was another emotion bubbling away.

'Did you see what he did?' she said.

'Who?'

'Bernard. Did you see?'

'No,' I said.

She shook her head angrily. 'He won't get away with it. I won't let him.'

'What?' I said. 'What did he do?'

While I waited for an answer that didn't come, I became aware that the silence held another sinister significance. Behind us, in the darkness of the cave, the goats had stopped calling.

My ankle, which hadn't bothered me at all on the ascent, was severely tested by the rapid downhill scramble back to the shack, and by the time we got there I could no longer disguise the fact that I was favouring it. Lobsang scolded me for keeping quiet about it and made me take off my boot, despite the cold, so that he could strap it up again.

Tenpa was nearby, rooting through his bag for something we could eat. I took the opportunity to ask one of the questions that was uppermost in my mind.

'How did Tenpa come to befriend the yeti?'

Lobsang passed on his answer. 'He comes from one of the villages we passed through. When he was a teenager he was very troubled. He had nightmares, hearing strange, sad voices in his head. His parents could not help him and they took him to the monastery. The monks there adopted him and taught him how to understand the workings of his mind. But the night voices did not leave him. Then, one day, a visiting abbot came to the monastery. He listened to Tenpa's story and told him to stop trying to rid himself of the voices and to follow them instead. He did. Up into the mountains. It was the yetis he had been hearing all those years. In the same way as he found your brother

243

and the little fox on the hill-side, he had found the yetis and heard their sorrow.'

I nodded. 'There were more of them then?'

Lobsang asked Tenpa. 'Yes. This one and her mother. Now her mother is dead.'

Tenpa shared out some salty fistfuls of roasted grain, and by the time we had finished chewing them he was already snoring loudly, wrapped in a single woollen blanket. As the rest of us wriggled into our sleeping bags and arranged ourselves around the driest bits of the floor, I wondered how he felt. He must have had great hopes that we could help the yeti. I was certain that he wouldn't have brought us with him if he had not. But if he was disappointed he gave no sign of it.

Slowly but surely the temperature inside my sleeping bag began to rise. I was hoping to wait until the others had all gone to sleep, but the longer I waited the clearer it became that it wasn't going to happen. Everyone except Tenpa seemed to be awake, sighing and shifting on the cold floor, wrestling mentally with the impossibility of what they had just seen.

Eventually I braced myself, slithered out of the cosy bag and pulled on my jacket and gloves.

'Are you all right, Christie?' asked Bernard, softly.

'Yeah,' I said, trying to sound exasperated. 'Just my bladder.'

Outside a half moon had risen and was

brightening the snows. When I was far enough from the hut I slipped the axe head from my pocket and examined it. The highly polished surface shone in the moonlight and I tried to imagine what kind of primitive process had wrought it. I had seen stone age tools in a Dublin museum, but nothing as perfectly preserved as this one.

What did you do with the only treasure of a lost people? The responsibility weighed heavily on me. I looked out beyond the glistening peaks to where the stars shone with a brilliance that they never had at home. I tried to remember what it was all about; the yeti, the missing link, the man with the rainbow arms and the space helmet. None of it made sense.

Lobsang had told me that the Buddhists believe desire is the cause of all suffering. At that moment I thought he was probably right. My head was full of desires; all of them conflicting. I wanted to be here, astonished by the sky and the snow, and I wanted to be at home, under my cosy quilt. I wanted to see the yeti again and I wished I had never seen her; never been burdened with the knowledge of her loneliness and the imminent extinction of her race. I wanted to keep her stone safe for all eternity, and I wished that she had chosen someone else for the job.

But she hadn't.

In my other pocket was the light scarf I used to protect my mouth and nose during blizzards.

I wrapped the stone in it and zipped it securely into an inside pocket. For the moment, at least, there was nothing else I could do.

10

Three days later, Lobsang appeared at the door of our room in the monastery. He was in a state of nervous excitement and told us to dress ourselves in our best clothes. The abbot, the head of the monastery, had offered us an audience, and we were to come as quickly as we could.

My ankle was better again and Roxy, though he had lost several of his pads and toes, seemed to be getting by all right without them. We all scurried around, shaking out our clothes, brushing our hair, washing our hands and faces. When we were finally as ready as we were ever going to be, Lobsang led us across the monastery to the audience chamber. Outside the door we were all given white silk scarves as offerings to the abbott. Then we were ushered in, like children who had been sent for by the head teacher.

The abbott sat cross-legged on a low wooden seat and smiled heartily as we came in. Lobsang prostrated himself and Bernard, after offering his scarf, followed suit. The rest of us felt that this wasn't the occasion to be practising moves like that, and the abbott seemed quite content with our scarves and hand-shakes. As we arranged ourselves on the floor around his feet, Lobsang told him our names, then retired, leaving us alone with the boss.

It turned out that the abbott's English was fluent. Lobsang told us later that he had been born into a wealthy Lhasa family and had studied medicine in London for several years before giving up his comfortable material existence to become a monk.

'I have been hearing all kinds of stories about you,' he said to us. 'Is it possible that they are true?'

'Well,' Bernard began, but the abbott didn't wait for his answer.

'Can you talk, little dog?' he said to Loki. 'Say something to me.'

But Loki, for some reason, had taken a dislike to the man, and slunk around behind me, mumbling under her breath.

'Pomp-monkey. Baldipate.'

I cleared my throat loudly, hoping the abbott wouldn't hear her, and Roxy stepped into the breach. He cringed and squirmed, as obsequious as only a fox can be. 'My most humble respects to your noble majesty.'

The abbott roared with laughter. 'How delightful! My respects to you also, my little red friend. But I am nobody's majesty. Not even my own!'

Loki started to grumble again and I gave her a dig with my elbow.

'We would like to thank you,' Bernard was saying. But again, the abbott cut him short.

'Yes, yes,' he said. 'But I am far too curious for a man of my age and position. I have heard about fish hearts and frog hearts and miraculous escapes from the snow. I want to know everything. Everything there is to know.'

There was a childlike glee in his face as he listened to Bernard's words. And, in a humble, trusting manner that I had never seen before, Bernard did as he had asked, and told him everything, right down to the search for the origins of the missing link and the reason we had come to Tibet. To my surprise he even told him about Danny, and how he had come to be lost at sea. When he came to the end of the story, the abbott sat back and appeared to fall asleep.

I wondered whether we ought to slip out and glanced at the others questioningly. But before we could make up our minds the abbott's eyes opened again and fixed upon Bernard.

'You are a clever man,' he said, 'and you have achieved a lot. But I have to admit that this . . .' he searched for the right word and found it. ' . . .this manipulation of nature makes me uneasy. There is so much trouble in the world because of it. And still you are searching for more.'

'I'm not really searching for trouble,' said Bernard.

'But you have found it and you are certain to find more of it as well. Because I see that you will not stop until you do.'

Bernard said nothing. The abbott turned to Sandy and Colin, who were sitting together. 'How does it feel to have the genes of other creatures in your bodies? Are you pleased with the results of your parents' experiments?'

Brother and sister looked at one another, clearly uneasy with the question. I wondered if anyone, in all of their lives, had ever asked it before. Colin answered first.

'I wouldn't be alive today if I didn't have the fish gene,' he said. 'It saved my life.'

The abbott nodded and turned his eyes to Sandy. She stared at the floor and, when it was clear that she wasn't going to make any reply, the abbott glanced briefly at Bernard, and said, 'Well, I suppose that not everybody can be happy. And you?'

A few moments passed before I realised that he was talking to me.

'Oh,' I said. 'I'm not . . . I mean . . . I'm like Bernard. I'm only human.'

'Ah,' said the abbott, as though I had told him something deeply revealing. 'Only human. How many times have I heard that expression? I couldn't help what I did. I'm only human. I may have made mistakes, but I'm only human. As though being human were a weakness.' He was gazing at me intently as he spoke, and although his words were intensely serious, his eyes were bright with humour and compassion. 'But what does it really mean to be only human, eh? Tenpa is only human and look at what he can do. Think about it, Christie. Think about what it might mean for humanity if being only human were not taken as an excuse for weakness and self-indulgence, but as the challenge it ought to be. After all, the Buddha himself was not a god, like Jesus or Krishna. He, too, was only human.'

I don't think any words had ever had such an effect upon me. My heart seemed to swell, not with pride but with possibility. To be the best that we could be, wasn't that all that anyone could ever wish for?

But my thoughts were bulldozed aside by the abbott's next words. As though he had changed gear, he became business-like, almost abrupt. 'It is time for you to leave the monastery. We have heard that the Chinese are coming to pay us a visit. You must be gone before they come.'

'Yes, of course,' said Bernard. 'We'll leave immediately.'

'Tomorrow morning will be soon enough,' said the abbott. The monk he had sent off earlier had returned, carrying a pile of white scarves. The abbott invited us forward, and one at a time we bent our heads to allow him to drape the fine silk around our necks. Roxy got one too, wound several times around him, but when it was Loki's turn to receive one she darted forward, grabbed the scarf from the abbott's hands and worried it around the tiled floor like a terrier with a rat. I closed my eyes, mortified, but the abbott was roaring with laughter again.

'This dog has been studying Zen,' he said. 'If you meet the Buddha on the road, kill him.'

He threw the last scarf at Hushy, plunging him into darkness and sending him instantly to sleep. 'But we Tibetans are not of the Zen school. You should not let the other monks see this.'

I retrieved the tattered scarf from Loki and, not knowing what else to do with it, stuffed it under my jumper.

'May I thank you now?' said Bernard.

'It is not necessary,' said the abbott.

'All the same,' said Bernard, 'we have never come across such kindness and generosity. If there is anything I can do to repay you, please ask.'

The abbott nodded, as though he had been expecting the question.

'It is so kind of you, so thoughtful, to ask for my permission before bestowing a gift upon me.'

11

'What did he mean?' said Bernard, when we were back in our rooms. 'Why did he thank me like that. For nothing, you know? What do you think he was talking about?'

I shrugged and began sorting through the heap of clothes that had accumulated on top of the ornate trunk in the corner.

But Sandy faced up to him squarely. 'You know exactly what he meant,' she said. 'You just don't want to hear, do you?'

'Hear what? I don't know what you're talking about,' said Bernard. But it was significant, I felt, that he chose that moment to go looking for Lobsang and didn't wait for an answer.

Lobsang and Tenpa joined us for our last evening in the monastery. We sat around the fire, all of us a little wistful about our imminent departure.

'Will you return home contented?' asked Lobsang. 'Have you found the answers to your questions in Tibet?'

I nodded, assuming that we had achieved more than we could ever have hoped for, in meeting the yeti. But no one else responded, and when I came to think about it more thoroughly, I realised that we hadn't; not really. We had established that the yeti must carry the missing link gene, but we were no closer to learning where it came from.

Tenpa looked across at me, his eyes twinkling with youthful mischief. Lobsang translated what he said. 'How strange human beings are. The harder they work to attain knowledge, the less of it they seem to acquire.'

Bernard laughed. 'That's Buddhism for you. Look no further than the view from your window if you want to attain wisdom.'

Lobsang laughed as well, but when Tenpa learned what Bernard had said he didn't laugh. Instead he looked long and hard at him. 'Beneath one's own nose may not be the last place one should look,' he said. 'But it makes sense that it should be the first.'

PART TEN

1

Maggie watched Danny like a hawk over the next few days. He was lean and fit from his weeks of swimming the oceans, and he threw himself vigorously into the daily routine of Fourth World. The stomach cramps and nausea that he had experienced when he first came home had already passed by the time the radiation theory arose, and Danny said nothing about them. They were, he knew, a result of his sudden change of diet, and there was no point in alarming his mother.

He was glad to be with her and Tina again, but although he realised how badly they needed his help, he also knew that every day that passed was a kind of betrayal. He was afraid that the merpeople would lose faith in him. Worse than that, he was afraid that they would grow tired of waiting for him and that he would never see them again.

Each evening, after the work was done, he would plead with Maggie to allow him to go. Tina looked on, constantly surprised by the arguments. If she had been Danny, she would have just gone. But it wasn't in Danny's nature to behave like that.

In the end, Tina got Maggie on her own one morning and talked to her about it.

'You can't keep him here. Or at least, you can, but you'll break his heart. He'll come to hate you.'

Maggie already knew it. 'I'm just afraid that he'll never come back,' she said. 'There's a wildness in him, Tina, have you seen it? Not wild the way all teenagers are. I mean wild like those creatures he wants to go back to. It's as though he's not . . .not entirely human any more.'

Tina was tempted to ask whose fault that might be, but she refrained. 'But you must understand how he feels. About the radiation sickness. About warning the others. Wouldn't you want to do the same thing, if you were him?'

Maggie's shoulders slumped. 'Of course I would. But I still can't let him go.'

'Maybe you have to,' said Tina. 'But you can make him promise to come back.'

Maggie knew that Tina was right. That evening she sat down with Danny and they had a long, long talk. Maggie took him back through the years of his life, from his genesis to his arrival at Fourth World, as though to imprint upon him the case for belonging. She made him talk about his memories and his feelings and his abilities; the positive things about his human side. While they talked, Tina was busy with a little project of her own. From a square of mustard-coloured linoleum left over from tiling the kitchen floor she cut a neat disc and painstakingly carved out the triple-winged radioactivity symbol. It was a long-shot. There was no guarantee that the radioactive leak was advertising itself, and nobody knew whether or not the sea people used or understood symbols. But it was, they all agreed, worth the effort. When she was satisfied with it, Tina bored a hole in one side, strung a boot-lace through it, and hung it round Danny's neck like some strange kind of talisman.

Night had fallen several hours ago. Now that Danny had been given permission to return to the sea, he wasted no time in setting out. His weed belt had dried and hardened in the days that he had been ashore, so he carried his harpoon in his hand as he walked away from Fourth World and vanished into the misty glen. Tina watched the empty path long after he had gone, deep in thought. The long hair and the harpoon were reminding her of something, and before she returned to the house, the first outlines of a strange theory were beginning to form in her mind.

2

The monks lent us a guide to lead us back over
the Himalayas to Nepal; a quiet young man
called Tsering. We had been lucky the last time,
Lobsang said, and I, for one, was all too willing
to agree with him.

It still wasn't easy, and I had to hide my
recurring ankle problems as well as I could from
the others. But with Tsering leading the way, it
was a much quicker and less hazardous journey
than the one we had undertaken on the way in.

After he left us, we walked through Nepal for
five days before we came to a proper, metalled
road. Sandy had a lot of trouble readjusting to
being in hiding. On one occasion a particularly
brave child, carrying out a dare perhaps, rushed
up to her and lifted her veil. Other than his
terrified retreat, no harm was done. But to
prevent it happening again she took to wearing
the veil over Colin's baseball cap, and gathering
it around her neck with the abbot's silk scarf. It
made her look like a mad beekeeper, but she
told us that it did a great job of keeping off
the mosquitos. Other than that, the only real

problem we encountered was not with people, but with dogs. Several times the local mutts took a dislike to us and decided to clear us from their territory. At the best of times it's pretty unpleasant being chased by dogs, but when there's the added danger of rabies, it's an experience I wouldn't wish on my worst enemy.

Loki didn't help. In her usual perverse manner, she seemed determined to thwart us, and took up with a scrawny, yellow dog who attached himself to us. We shouted and threw stones at him, but he was as persistent as the blazing sun and refused to leave us alone.

To make matters even worse, Loki was constantly sneaking off to join him and romp around the fields. I told her a hundred times to stay away, but she always forgot, whether accidentally or on purpose I couldn't be sure. She seemed to be blind to his very obvious faults, and called him 'Splendid-chap', 'Companero', and other completely inappropriate names. One night she ate her way out of the tent, and Hushy woke me up to raise the alarm. I called and called, waking the entire party, but I didn't see her again until the following morning when she turned up at the camp, covered in dust and looking extremely guilty.

Eventually I put Loki on a lead and didn't let her out of my sight for a minute. The following day we arrived at a metalled road and were back on to the crowded and hair-raising buses again.

Sandy coped well with the unashamed curiosity of our fellow passengers, and Colin, though visibly uncomfortable, didn't complain once about the heat. But Bernard was like a cat on a hot tin roof for the whole time we were travelling across India and Nepal. When we left the bus routes to find a quiet border crossing, he marched us like a troop of squaddies on a training drill. When the buses and trains were late, as they usually were, or when they stopped for long periods, as they usually did for inexplicable reasons, he nearly tore his hair out. Several times he engaged in senseless running battles with drivers and ticket collectors, and on one occasion he made us all walk along the sunbaked railway tracks, in the conviction that it would be quicker. When, soon afterwards, the train passed us by, he hurled rocks after it until it was out of sight.

3

To Danny's relief, the merpeople were still waiting and they came to him at dawn, a mile or so off shore. They were pleased to see him, but were disappointed when he made the sign for death, to tell them that he had failed to save the child. Her parents, who had waited along with the others, were devastated. They pulled and dragged at Danny, desperate to have her body, until he demonstrated, by piling rocks on the seabed, that she had been safely buried. It was a lie, but for their sakes as well as his own, it was one that he felt obliged to tell.

For a while everyone stayed around the symbolic cairn, making the sign for sorrow and going through the funeral ritual, even though they had no body. Then, when they appeared to have become reconciled to the loss, Danny drew everyone's attention to his pendant. But the merpeople could not have been less interested if he had shown them an empty oyster shell. The radioactivity symbol was meaningless to them.

The waters were bitterly cold and the merpeople wasted no time in setting out for the south. They travelled in their usual way, fishing and browsing along the continental shelf, and Weaver made Danny a new belt on the way, to relieve him of the trouble of carrying his harpoon. Danny swam with him for a while, pleased to be back, enjoying his return to the diet which, he now understood, suited him far better than the one he had been obliged to endure for most of his life. But as he went, he kept a close eye on the dead child's parents, and when they began to drift apart from the others he stayed with them. If Maggie was right about the radioactive leak, it was sure to be somewhere near their feeding grounds.

Before the day was out, he had lost contact with his own clan. No one, not even Mrs No-No, had bothered to follow him. For the first time he was uncertain about their fellowship, and it crossed his mind that they had lost interest in him now that the novelty of his arrival had worn off.

For two days Danny stayed with the grieving couple as they swam steadily southward. Then, on the morning of the third day, they made aural contact with some members of their tribe, and soon they were met by another couple, moving fast towards them, carrying yet another sick child to find Danny and Mrs No-No.

Danny was moved to see that, despite his consistent failure with their children, they still held him in trust. He knew that he couldn't help, and he also knew now that he was putting himself at risk, but he took the young boy in his arms anyway, and stroked his little head. Anchored by its bootlace, the pendant floated in the water close to the child's face. To Danny's surprise, a spark of interest came into his impassive eyes, and he lifted a finger and pointed at the symbol.

It wasn't much. The gesture could have meant anything or nothing. But it fired Danny's resolve and, by setting out again, he demonstrated with the others that he wanted them to take him to their home.

4

Danny's little group of friends joined the rest of
their clan in the Celtic Sea, south of Ireland and
west of Cornwall. A number of shallow banks
gave diversity to the habitat, and the merpeople
were clearly well established there.

But they were not happy. By the time Danny's
party arrived, two more of the children were
already seriously ill and others were showing
less severe but nonetheless worrying symptoms.

Danny was tired after the long swim and had
hoped to be able to rest for a while before beginning his exploration of the area. But it wasn't
to be. His pendant had caused an immediate
flurry of excitement among the healthy children,
and they swarmed around him, competing for
his attention. One of the girls pushed forward,
pointing at the pendant and then at something
unseen in the far-distant depths. She made the
sign for following, and Danny relinquished the
child that he had been carrying into the care of
his parents. At his signal, the merchildren burst
away like a cloud of minnows, then back-tracked
and trod water, waiting for him to catch up.

For a mile or so, they stayed close to the

surface, popping up as and when they needed to breathe. But then they all surfaced together, drawing Danny with them. He had seen this joint action among the merpeople before. It always happened when everyone was about to dive together.

And this time was no exception. Down they went, down to the level of the shell-fish rich banks and beyond, into the deeper and darker waters below. Neither the pressure nor the distance bothered Danny, but he knew that if they went much deeper he wouldn't be able to see what it was they were so keen to show him. But just at the limits of his eyesight the sunken ship came into view.

Danny hesitated, then stopped swimming and began to drift upwards. To his relief, the children noticed and converged on him again. They pointed and tugged at the pendant clearly implying that they had seen the same symbol somewhere aboard the ship. But he pulled free and shook his head and made the wide-eyed danger signs that he knew they would understand, and the sad-faced death sign that he had already witnessed too many times. The children looked doubtful, then disappointed, and then, finally, Danny saw the truth begin to dawn upon their innocent faces. The smart, modern ship, such a brilliant place to explore, was the source of the mysterious illness.

Their favourite playground was killing them.

5

When at last we arrived at Vijay's village, the reason for Bernard's anxiety became apparent. He didn't even put his rucksack down before he rushed round the side of the house and on to the beach. I followed and, by the time I reached him, saw that the worry had already gone from his face. He was relaxed and smiling, gazing out into the bay at the love of his life.

And there she lay; *The Privateer*, as calm and serene and as tidy and trim as she had been on the day we left.

We spent a couple of days gathering supplies to restock the boat for our journey home. Vijay was invaluable; it seemed as though, provided the price was right, there was nothing on earth that he couldn't lay his hands on. He even dredged up a ship's radio from somewhere; not new, but in perfect working order.

Meanwhile, the rest of us lounged around, enjoying Ruma's hospitality. She was still very frightened of Sandy and wouldn't come within arm's reach of her. I know it bothered Sandy, but she endured it in silence.

The yeti's stone had become a problem for me as soon as it had become warm enough to take off my down jacket. It was too big to go into the pocket of my jeans and I was reluctant to let it out of my sight until it was securely stashed away somewhere. Nor did I want to draw attention to the fact that I had something precious by starting, at this late stage of the journey, to carry a small bag. There was nothing for it in the end but to leave it where it was in the pocket of my jacket, and to stuff the whole lot into the rucksack. I was still anxious, though, and when we boarded *The Privateer* the first thing I did as I stowed my gear was feel for the stone in the jacket pocket.

It was still there; still wrapped in the scarf. And there it would stay, as far as I was concerned, until we got home to Fourth World. I was itching to get a proper daylight look at it, but the boat was too small. The chances of being spotted were way too high.

In any case, before twenty-four hours were out, we were all too concerned with sailing the boat to worry about what was in each other's pockets. Or so I thought. What I didn't know at the time was that I wasn't the only one who had something precious and secret tucked away.

6

Danny left the people of the Celtic Sea and set off for the north again, hoping to find his own clan before they had gone too far south. He was satisfied with what he had achieved. Although he could do nothing for the children who were already dead or dying, he was certain that the tribe had understood the danger and would change their feeding grounds when they returned to the north the following year.

He swam hard, resting only to eat and get brief snatches of rest. Without the others to take turns on watch it was dangerous to sleep at sea. Sharks were scarce in these waters but people weren't, and Danny lived in fear of being seen.

At every familiar feeding ground that he passed, Danny watched out carefully for signs of his friends. But they were nowhere. His heart began to grow heavy. He knew that they could find him if they wanted to. Perhaps they didn't. Perhaps they were watching him even now, getting on with their hidden lives, waiting for him to get on with his and leave them alone. For three more days Danny swam around the waters off the west coast of Ireland but the seas were cold and windswept and lonely, and there was clearly no hope to be had there.

As he turned his head towards home, Danny was heartbroken. He was sure now that the mer-people had abandoned him. He loved them too much to be angry. If they had rejected him there had to be a reason, and he knew what it was. He had taken the merchild ashore; broken one of their inviolable rules. And he hadn't brought her back.

PART ELEVEN

1

In the days after Danny left, Maggie noticed that Tina seemed to be quieter and more thoughtful than was usual for her. One morning she found her in the sitting room, examining the photographs that had been lying there since the day Bernard showed them to the family. When Maggie asked her why, she put them away again.

'Just curious,' she said.

But that evening when they were sitting in the kitchen, finally stringing the onions, Tina gave a clue to the direction her thoughts were taking.

'Did you do any genetic testing on that sea-creature?'

Maggie shook her head. 'I will, some day,' she said. 'If I ever find myself with time on my hands.'

They both knew the likelihood of that and Tina said, 'I'd take over for a day or two. I'd like to know what you come up with.'

Maggie laid a hand on her belly, drawing Tina's attention to its increasing size. 'I'm not too keen on handling any more radioactive material just now, if I can avoid it,' she said. 'What is it you want to know?'

Tina shrugged. 'It's nothing, really. I just think it's strange. They must be related to us, mustn't they? In some way?'

'They certainly look as if they might be,' said Maggie. 'It's been making me think as well.'

'About what?'

'Well, there was a theory, which tends to be ignored, that human beings spent some part of their evolution in the sea. There's a certain amount of evidence to suggest that it might be true.'

Tina put the onions down and leant forward, her eyes bright and keen. 'Like what?'

'For one thing, new babies can swim as soon as they're born. It seems to be instinctive. And for another, why have we got so little hair on our bodies? What happened to it?'

'We didn't need it in the sea,' said Tina.

'That's the theory anyway,' said Maggie. 'And we have much more subcutaneous fat than most land species.'

'To keep us warm underwater,' said Tina.

Maggie nodded. 'It has even been suggested that we learnt to walk upright in the sea. To keep our heads above water. But you know, there's something even stranger than that.'

'What?' said Tina.

'Well, you know that Danny always had that amazing ability to hold his breath?'

'Yes.'

276

'That was one of the reasons I knew that the dolphin genes were active in his constitution. He did it naturally, of course. But it's possible that we could all hold our breath for as long as that, if we got into training at a young enough age.'

'Wow,' said Tina.

'The record for a human being holding their breath underwater is over seven minutes. That's as long as a dolphin can.'

Tina nodded and fell silent, but Maggie could see that she was tense with excitement. She knew the feeling; she had been there many times herself; the researcher on the verge of a great discovery. It was precious and not to be disturbed. When Tina was good and ready, she would share what she was thinking.

2

Danny came home a few days later, exhausted and dispirited. He slept for twenty-four hours, then got up and joined in the daily rounds of Fourth World life.

When Maggie asked him how things had worked out, he told her about the ship he had found. But he didn't seem as pleased as he should have been, and he made no more mention of the sea and its occupants. Nor, to Maggie's disappointment, did he resume his nightly fishing trips. It was as though he had put the ocean behind him and wanted to forget that it existed.

Maggie did her best to cheer him up and he did his best to respond. But it was clear that he wasn't the same old carefree Danny who had set out on *The Privateer* so many months ago.

There was nothing that Maggie or anyone else could do to relieve his sorrow, but she worried about him anyway. At night she often lay awake, thinking about her children and the strange burdens they all had to carry through life. She blamed herself, and searched her soul long into the small hours, wondering whether she and

Bernard had been right to do what they had done. And the only conclusion that gave her any peace was that there was nothing they could do about it now. Everyone would just have to make the best of who, or what, they were.

Including the newcomers. She turned heavily on to her side and wished that Danny or Tina would say something to her; allow her to bring it out into the open. Surely they must have noticed by now?

3

Late one night a few weeks later, the patrol dogs started barking. Maggie switched on her light and looked at her watch. It was four o'clock.

For a few minutes she lay rigid in bed, listening to the growing fury of the dogs. Surely it was nothing; another false alarm. A stray dog or a fox around the hen-house or . . .

But a sudden, dreadful sound put an end to her musings and sent her, despite her bulk, leaping out of bed and on to the landing. Out in the darkness, someone had fired a gun. The worst of Maggie's fears was about to be realised.

Itchy came racing back to the house to raise the alarm. Maggie met her at the back door.

'Bad men,' she jabbered.

'How many?' said Maggie.

'Lots. Twenty. Thirty. They shot Obi, Mother.'

'Oh, God,' said Maggie. 'Call off the rest of the dogs. Don't let anyone else get hurt.'

Itchy raced off just as Tina appeared in her pyjamas.

'What's happening?'

'Paramilitaries,' said Maggie. 'Get Danny, quick. And get some boxes of food organised.'

Tina didn't wait to be told twice. Maggie ran out to the yard, flinging open all the outhouse doors and yelling at the frightened animals.

'Get out! Run for your lives!'

'Where?' said one of Iggy's daughters. 'Why?' said another. They were full-grown pigs now, and the whole brood had inherited their mother's tendency to avoid exercise whenever possible.

'Just go!' screamed Maggie. 'Far away from here. Keep going and don't look back. There are men coming and if they catch you they'll kill you!'

As well as the pigs there was a new generation of young goats and assorted descendants of wild creatures in the outbuildings. All of them had been bred in Fourth World and all of them had the ability to speak. Galvanized by Maggie's panic, they scattered across the yard and vanished into the darkness beyond.

Back in the kitchen, Maggie loaded Tina and Danny with supplies and gave them the key to the lab.

'What about you?' said Danny.

'I'm coming. Now go on!'

There were voices in the distance and, as Maggie scrambled around collecting essentials, Darling came diving in through the open door.

'Obi's dead,' she said. 'They're coming! They're nearly at the glen gate!'

'Keep yourselves safe,' said Maggie, running out, her arms full. 'Tell the dogs to stay clear! Keep your eye on what's happening here and send us messages through Klaus.'

'Through Klaus. I will. Take care!'

Then Darling was gone, soaring up into the trees. A moment later, Maggie was hurrying down the steps which led to the lab, and closing the trap door behind her.

5

Maggie and Danny and Tina were safe enough in the lab complex. For an outsider there was no way of knowing that the place existed, let alone that there were people in there. They had water and food and, although it wasn't exactly warm, the place was well enough insulated by the surrounding earth to be tolerably comfortable.

It was an awful time for them nonetheless. Above their heads, Fourth World was being ravaged and there was nothing at all they could do about it.

Klaus brought regular reports. The men were eating their way through all the frozen and bottled food. They couldn't be bothered, it seemed, to pick the fresh greens that were still plentiful in the garden, though they had discovered the potato clamp and had plundered it, leaving the potatoes they didn't eat scattered around for the slugs and the crows and the rats. They were working their way through the chickens, slaughtering a few every day. But despite all the food they had, they wouldn't spare anything for the dogs. One by one they were deserting Fourth World and setting off to find someone who would feed them.

'You know what bothers me most,' said Tina, voicing a fear that they all privately held. 'Why would they ever want to leave? A big house, a perfect fortress for them. Loads of food.'

'It won't last them that long,' said Maggie. 'Especially the way they're going.'

'Maybe not. But they might figure out how to grow it. Or just raid the neighbours for it.'

And still the news got worse. 'They killed the jersey heifers,' Klaus reported. 'And when they couldn't catch Tony they tried to shoot him. He jumped out and got away. I don't think they hit him.'

'Oh no,' said Tina. 'Poor Tony.'

'Darling says Kanobi and Sparky are hanging round Obi's body and won't leave him. They're getting very thin.'

Klaus went quiet while Maggie and the others absorbed what he had told them. Then, before he left, he said, sadly, 'They're making an awful mess of the place, Mother. I'm glad you can't see what they've done.'

6

The radio made life aboard *The Privateer* a lot easier, and although Albert didn't track us down again, we managed to steer clear of trouble. The trade winds were behind us all the way up the African coast, and though they often blew harder than we might have wished, *The Privateer* weathered the storms with unruffled fortitude.

Her crew weathered them just as well. In some ways we were at our best when there was a crisis to be confronted. It was the quiet times, the stretches of plain sailing which were the worst. None of us could ignore the continuing cold war between Bernard and Sandy, which escalated by the day and the week. By the time we reached the offshore waters of Portugal, they were not speaking to each other at all.

Unaccountably, Loki got seasick, and Colin developed a high temperature for a few days which had us all worried. But they both recovered, relieving us of the necessity of going ashore, and in two months of travelling we never set eye upon land.

As we neared the west coast of Ireland I put in a request with Bernard to be allowed to pay a brief visit to my mother and stepfather. He considered it for a while, but eventually turned it down.

'We've been away nearly eight months,' he said. 'There's no knowing what might be happening at Fourth World.'

I was partly disappointed and partly relieved. I would have loved to see them again, but I was dreading the prospect of breaking the news about Danny.

7

It was late morning on the ninth day of Fourth World's occupation when Klaus brought the amazing news.

'They're gone!' he said. 'No one knows why. One minute they were all lounging around in the kitchen and the next, three or four of them came running in from outside and said they were pulling out. They were white as sheets and shaking. The others went out, and when they came back they were looking pretty peaky as well. Then they all threw their things together and went off. Very quickly.'

'Are you sure, Klaus?' said Tina. 'Are you sure they've really gone?'

'As sure as I can be.'

'Maybe the army's coming,' said Tina. 'Have the birds seen anything?'

'No reports,' said Klaus.

Everyone fell silent for a few moments, puzzling over the unexpected development. Then Klaus said, 'Well? Are you coming out or not?'

He was right about the mess. Every pot and pan and plate and cup in the kitchen was either dirty or smashed. The oat-bin had been emptied and used for rubbish, and was overflowing with rotting leftovers, stinking to high heaven. Chicken feathers were everywhere, drifted up in the corners, floating on currents of air, getting into everyone's mouth and nose and under their clothes, reminding them of the comfortable, well-tended birds that had so recently owned them.

Almost all of the bottled food had been plundered. The freezer in the scullery was empty and the floor was strewn with containers and lids, many of them trampled and broken. Tina went upstairs and found that it was just as bad up there. Bedding was strewn everywhere and dirty clothes that had been left behind in the sudden rush to get out. To her relief, she found the folder containing Bernard's photographs was still where she had left it, on the floor beside her bed. She checked its contents, then began to sort out the bedclothes. Nestled among the folds of her quilt, darker and more deadly than a poisonous snake, she found a rifle. For a long time she stood and stared at it, knowing the way Maggie felt about guns, knowing what she would do if she knew it was there. Filled with guilt, but determined nonetheless to keep it, Tina hid it under her mattress and continued with her tour of the house.

Darling floated into the kitchen and perched above the filthy range.

'They're gone,' she said. 'Way off along the main road. Going fast, too.'

'Do you know where any of the animals are?' said Maggie.

'Hiding,' said Darling. 'Some of them have disappeared completely. Too far away to find them.'

'Tell anyone you see that it's safe to come back,' said Maggie.

Tina and Danny went down the glen to bury what remained of Obi. Kanobi and Sparky were still there; thin and weak, but overjoyed to see them. Although they couldn't speak, they seemed to appreciate what Danny and Tina were doing and waited with them until the last shovelfuls of earth had been thrown on to the grave.

They were just about to return to Fourth World when a familiar voice greeted them from the trees above.

'Is that Danny, is that Danny? I thought you were dead, were dead, were dead.'

Maggie, meanwhile, was investigating the farm buildings. There were still a few thin, terrified chickens cowering in the hen-house, but it would be a long time before they started laying again, and it would be even longer before the numbers could be brought up to their previous level. The milking cows both had mastitis, since none of the intruders had known how to milk them, and they were traumatized by the stench of their daughters' rotting hides and guts, which had been slung on to the manure heap. Maggie was glad they couldn't talk and that she wouldn't have to hear about what they had witnessed. With care and kindness they would recover, but whether they would ever completely trust people again remained to be seen.

She spent a gruelling half hour burying the calves' skins and innards. The muck heap was wet and heavy after three weeks of rain, and it was like moving around in a deep, slimy bog. By the time she had finished Maggie was soaked to the skin and filthy, but the smell of manure was many times sweeter than the stench of decomposing offal. Since she was wet already, she turned the hose on herself and sluiced down her clothes before setting off back to the house.

On her way, she passed through the yard and looked into each of the buildings, one by one. In the old stable, she found the reason for the sudden departure of the makeshift army.

Clearly they had been looking for more food and had come across the other freezer humming away in the corner. Inside it they had found a large, plastic-wrapped parcel and had dragged it out on to the floor and torn it open. Even though Maggie had seen the merchild before, the sight of her thawing corpse in the dim shed sent a chill tide through her blood. She could well understand how even grown men would have been horror-struck by the sight. It would

290

have turned their opinion of Fourth World on its head; made it seem like a ghost house, full of lurking terrors. If she had been them, she would have scarpered as well.

'What in God's name is that?'

The sound of a man's voice made Maggie whip round, ready to fight for her life. But she didn't have to. Standing in the doorway was Bernard and he was the most welcome sight she had ever seen in her life.

PART TWELVE

1

It was brilliant to see Danny again, alive and well and with amazing stories to tell. But our homecoming spirits were dampened by the chaos that met us in Fourth World. I suppose we had expected to be greeted as heroes returning from campaign, with Maggie and Tina full of welcome and admiration. But if any of us were heroes, it was them.

They had both changed enormously since we had last seen them. Tina was thinner than ever and looked much older, as though time had travelled here at a different speed. And Maggie was colossal; a mountain on legs. The sight of her embarrassed me. I hardly dared to look at her, unless she caught my eye and detected what I was thinking.

We were all exhausted, but there could be no thought of resting while the house was in such a state. So we put down our bags, rolled up our sleeves and ploughed into the work. We scrubbed the kitchen, took out the rubbish, scoured the bathrooms, washed the bedclothes; tried to wipe out all trace of the intruders and salvage what was left of our home.

By the time evening came there were still plenty of things to be done, but Maggie lit a fire in the sitting room and declared that we were all off duty. We sprawled around on the sofas and the floor, allowing the heat to melt the stiffness from our tired limbs, and before long the sense of violation that still hovered around the house began to recede. As our stories unfolded, Fourth World began to feel safe and its weird assortment of inhabitants were a family again, delighted to be reunited.

Throughout the day we had been gathering snatches of each other's stories, but there was still plenty left to be told. Danny filled us in on the merpeople and their tragic encounter with the wreck, and when he had finished, we took over. At the most exciting points, Loki would jump up and join in, saying things like 'Clamorous-tiger-storm,' and 'Gobbling-snow-thunder!' and she would chase Roxy around the room until he holed up under Bernard's armchair. I noticed that, while everyone else was as lean and skinny as church mice, she was considerably plump around the middle. Putting two and two together I ventured to ask her a question.

'Loki? Was that Nepali dog your boyfriend?'

'Dashing-cavalier!' she confirmed, happily, and made another excited circuit of the room.

'That'll be interesting,' said Colin. 'Talking pi-dogs.'

While we were describing our spell in the

monastery, Loki appeared to be asleep, but she woke up and listened attentively when we approached the climax and our meeting with the yeti.

Nothing we said would convince Tina we were telling the truth.

'Yeah, yeah, yeah,' she said. 'And we had centaurs dancing on the lawns at night, didn't we, Maggie?'

'Centaurs?' said Bernard. 'What have you been up to?'

Maggie shot him a mock-threatening look. 'Don't even think about it, pal.'

'Why didn't you bring it home, then?' Tina jeered.

'She didn't want us to,' said Sandy. 'She didn't trust the human race, you know?' She glanced at Bernard. 'And she was probably right.'

I stepped in to avert the brewing argument, and took up where we had left off. I told them more about the yeti and related the story she had told us. As Tina listened, the smirk gradually left her face.

'It fits,' she said at last.

'Fits what?' said Maggie.

Tina was so excited that she stumbled all over her words. 'The picture. The missing link. The helix man and the yeti and all that. I have a theory.'

'Really?' Bernard leant forward. 'Let's have it, then.'

Tina went upstairs to her room and brought down the pink folder, then sifted through the photographs until she came to the one that showed the whole rock carving. The rest of us gathered round.

'Look,' she said. 'This wavy line here, the one you thought was the bottom of the clouds. I don't think it is. I think it's the top of the sea.'

'I suppose it could be,' said Maggie.

'It is,' said Tina. 'It came to me when I saw Danny walking off that night, with his long hair and . . .' She pointed to the spear. The figure who held it had a dimple in his torso, and I remembered Loki dribbling on to it that night so long ago. What was it she had said? Something about swimming? Swimmeryman? She had said that again, I remembered, when Danny went overboard the night we lost him. I had ignored her; assumed that she was talking nonsense. She had known all along, but no one would listen to her. Poor Loki.

As Tina continued, her words sent a holy shiver up my spine.

'Don't you see? It's not a spear he's holding. Or at least, it is. But it's for fish, not for game. It's a harpoon.'

'It is!' said Danny.

'It could be,' said Bernard.

'What if it is?' said Colin.

'Well,' said Tina. 'Maggie says some people think we spent part of our lives in the sea. Part of our evolution, I mean. So what I think is . . .'

She paused, gathering her thoughts. 'What if the yeti's story is true? Except that the ones who got trapped by the sea didn't die. They adapted. It happened slowly, remember? Maybe they lived a kind of amphibious life – half in and half out of the water. Then, when the floods went down, some of them came out again, back on to the land.'

'And some of them didn't,' said Danny. 'Some of them stayed.'

'And became the merpeople,' said Maggie.

'Exactly,' said Tina. 'And when they came out, one of them made this carving. It shows it all, you see. The ape-people who stayed on land, on the high ground. The people who stayed in the sea and developed into merfolk.'

I had to admit it made a lot of sense. 'So what about the helix man?' I said. 'Where does he fit in?'

'I don't know,' said Tina. 'But he isn't floating in the clouds like you thought. He's right on the water-line. And it's not a flying saucer, it's a boat.'

Bernard was irritated, I could tell. 'But the helmet,' he said. 'That's pretty obvious, isn't it?'

'It's not a helmet, it's his hair,' said Tina. 'Like an afro. Around his head.'

I reached out for the photograph and studied it again.

'He's us, then,' I said.

All eyes turned to me, all, except Tina, with perplexed expressions.

'The helix man,' I went on. 'Maybe he's us. Standing in our boat, between the water and the land. You know, master of both of them. And the rainbow might just be a bow, for hunting, and the rays are arrows, some of them pointing towards the sea and some towards the land.' Only Tina was nodding. 'And the double helix . . .' I found it hard to say it.

'The double helix?' said Maggie.

'Maybe it is a double helix, and we are the result of someone else's experiment. And maybe it isn't. Maybe it's just a squiggle.'

2

In the quiet of the room everyone was suddenly alone, each of us immersed in our own thoughts. I was struggling with the emerging sense that it had all been for nothing; an absurd and dangerous wild goose chase, when Maggie took my reasoning a stage further.

'Pity the yeti didn't agree to being cloned. We might have been able to discover something more about them. Especially if they're the original. The model from which we all evolved.'

Bernard drew himself away from his own gloomy thoughts and brightened up a bit. 'We might be able to get around that.' He left the room and we all waited in suspense. But when he came back, his face was as white as the wall. 'I don't understand it,' he said. 'It was in my coat pocket.'

'Is this what you're looking for?'

Sandy was standing beside the fireplace, holding up a plastic film container. The last time I had seen it was in the yeti's cave.

'Where did you get that?' said Bernard.

'Just where you said. Your coat pocket.'

Bernard shook his head irritably and held out his hand for it. But Sandy didn't hand it over.

'No way,' she said. 'You're not doing this, Bernard. Not this time.'

'What are you talking about, Sandy? What do you think I'm going to do?'

'I saw you, you see,' said Sandy. 'While the yeti was talking to us. Trusting us, because Tenpa had told us she could. You betrayed her.' She opened the container and shook the contents on to her hand. Even as they spilled out, I could see the lush red glow of the yeti hairs. Tina and Maggie drew closer and examined them, but they might not have been there as far as Sandy was concerned.

'You had no right to take these,' she went on. 'You didn't deserve her trust.'

'Don't be so ridiculous, Sandy,' said Bernard. 'I'm not going to do any harm, you know that.'

'I know exactly what you're going to do. You're going to clone her, aren't you? Or make a human baby with yeti genes; another freak like me.'

'Of course I'm not!' Bernard was losing his cool. His voice was rising through the scale.

'That's what you say,' said Sandy. 'But you said that before. You swore, after the poor little bird baby was born, that you wouldn't make any more of us.' She turned and glared at Maggie. 'But you've broken your promise, both of you. Haven't you? Loki isn't the only one here who's expecting.'

I must have been mad or blind or both, not to have realised that Maggie's sudden expansion wasn't due to overeating. All the time she and Bernard had spent in the lab while we worked on *The Privateer*, this was what they had been doing. I stared into the fire. Maggie had given me the same assurance, when I first saw the lab. There were to be no more experiments.

'What is it this time?' Sandy was saying. 'A tarantula? A ferret?'

'That's enough, Sandy.' The colour was rushing back into Bernard's cheeks with dangerous speed. 'Give me that.'

Sandy held the hairs tight. 'Not in a million years.'

Bernard shook his head in disbelief. 'I don't understand. What is it with you, Sandy? How could you not trust your own father?'

'Because you don't act like a father! You don't treat us like children. You behave as though we're just interesting oddities that you created. You don't see that we have feelings too. You just don't care!'

Bernard turned away, but Sandy pursued him; stood in front of him. 'No. That's what you always do. It's easy, isn't it, to turn away and put it out of your mind. But I can't. Everywhere I go, people will stare at me, and that will never change. I'm a freak, Dad. I wish I'd never been born! I want you to look at me. Look at what you've made!'

'You are what you are, Sandy! We all are!'

'Stop!'

It was my own voice. I didn't remember giving it the go ahead, but something was rising so powerfully into my chest that it seemed to have happened without my will.

They did stop. I had to continue.

'We haven't learnt anything, have we? None of us. We've been to the top of the world and the depths of the sea, and we still haven't learnt.'

'Learnt what?' said Colin.

'The first thing. The most blindingly obvious thing of all.'

They waited. I wished it wasn't me who had to say it. 'What's the one thing they have in common, the merpeople and the yeti?'

'Language?' said Colin.

'The missing link?' said Maggie.

'They share some genes with us?' said Tina.

'Maybe,' I said. 'I wasn't thinking of any of those things, though. What struck me is that they're both afraid of us.' I paused, but no one had anything to say, so I went on. 'They've lived in hiding for thousands of years, knowing what would happen if they showed themselves to . . . to the guy on the boat. To us.'

'But you said it yourself, Christie,' said Bernard. 'You said it to the yeti. Maybe we've changed now.'

'We haven't, though, have we?' I said. 'We've only been back a day, and look at us. Fights. Deceptions. No one listening to each other.'

Bernard closed his eyes and clenched his jaw.

I thought I'd gone too far. I feared the explosion that seemed to be building, and I know I wasn't the only one. For a long minute Bernard stood like that, as if battling with some inner demon. Then, to my surprise, he looked up at me and nodded.

'You're right, Christie,' he said.

Then he turned to Sandy and did as she had asked. He looked at her small eyes, her long skull and high, sharp cheekbones, her dry, stretched skin. Then, at last, he dropped his eyes and placed a light hand on her shoulder.

'I'm sorry, Sandy. It's true that I didn't want to hear that you were unhappy. It undermined my beliefs. It made me unsure about what I was doing. If I haven't . . .'

He reached out and gripped her shoulder; the clearest sign of affection he had ever shown her. Then, while she was off guard, he pulled the trailing hairs from her fingertips.

3

Sandy stared at him, unable to believe that, even at a time like this he was prepared to betray her. He ran the fine hairs through his fingers and the firelight glinted off them; red on red. He had found what he had set out to find. A drop of blood or a hair or a toenail, he had said. All he needed to continue his research was safely in his hand.

Even Maggie was shocked. She leaned forward to speak, but changed her mind, as though she understood that what had started between Sandy and Bernard had to end with them as well.

'You're really going to do it, aren't you?' said Sandy. 'Nothing anyone says can touch you, can it?'

Bernard studied the gleaming strands. 'This is all there is,' he said. 'In a few year's time the yeti we met will be dead. We hold the key right here, the only chance there will ever be to reproduce her. Do you really think I was wrong to keep that possibility alive?'

I had been on Sandy's side until then, but now I wasn't so sure. It seemed so momentous;

such a dreadful responsibility for anyone to carry. But Sandy had no doubts.

'What I think doesn't matter. Or what you think, or anyone else in this room. What matters is her wishes. She made them clear to us, Dad. We don't have the right to ignore her.'

For a long, long time Bernard stood silently, observing the red-gold hairs. Then he looked up into Sandy's eyes again. 'Do you really wish you hadn't been born?' he said.

Sandy held his gaze. She thought for a moment, then said, 'No. What I wish is that I'd been born human. Only human. That's all.'

Bernard nodded sadly. Then, without a word, he leaned over and dropped the strands of hair into the flames.

There was a brief fizz, that was all, and the last chance to keep a yeti alive upon the face of the earth went up in smoke. In the same moment the tension between Sandy and Bernard evaporated, and, although they neither touched nor looked at each other, there was no doubt at all that something had changed between them. The rift ran too deep to be healed overnight, but I was as certain as I could be that, sooner or later, the two of them would become reconciled.

And as if in agreement with my unspoken thoughts, Loki sighed hugely and laid herself flat on the rug.

'Om mane padme hum,' she said.

4

The following morning Oggy returned, and throughout the day a few others came trickling home. One of the goats appeared with her kid, and Iggy, with one of her daughters. In the evening, Loki's brother Sam arrived in, but of the rest of her siblings and most of the pigs and of Tony there was no sign at all. The birds searched far and wide, but although they did manage to track down a few of the wild creatures, most of the animals who fled at the time that came to be known as The Invasion were never seen again in Fourth World.

The day was spent on more clearing and cleaning and repairing. We salvaged the remaining potatoes and put them back into storage and picked buckets of sprouts and broccoli to begin restocking the freezer. Sandy, in the best spirits I had ever seen her, treated the cows and cleaned out their filthy byre and bedded them down with mountains of soft, sweet oat straw. Danny and I dug a big pit and buried all the stinking rubbish, then scoured out the oat-bin with boiling water. Bernard and

Sandy, working quietly together, scrubbed the grease from the range and cleaned out the build-up of soot and ashes. When they lit it again it chugged away happily, like a heart that had been damaged and was now healed.

I'd spent the previous night in my sleeping bag on the sitting room floor, but I was keen to reclaim my own bed. I stripped the sheets and put on a fresh set. Then I unpacked.

The yeti's stone was still in my jacket pocket. I took another look at it, nestled in the folds of my scarf. The daylight showed me nothing more than the moonlight had, but nonetheless there was something nagging at the back of my mind. There had been no evidence to suggest that the yetis used tools of any kind. If they had done once, why didn't they now? Was there some other significance to the polished stone?

I wanted to share the responsibility with someone; Tina, maybe, or Danny. But there was no hurry. I wrapped it up again and pushed it under my mattress, then carried on unpacking.

By the time we had finished the first round of decontamination and managed to scrape together a meal, we were too tired even for stories and the only things we discussed were the invaders and their swift departure. The dead child was back in the freezer, and, since we had all had a good look at her, Maggie suggested that it was time to lay her to rest.

'We should bury her tomorrow,' she said. 'I've

got all the samples I need, and it's too dangerous to keep her there any longer.'

'Even though she saved Fourth World?' said Sandy.

'Even though she saved Fourth World,' said Maggie.

'Another grave,' said Tina. 'Bagsy I not do the digging.'

But there wasn't to be another grave. By morning, the corpse was gone.

Danny took her away in the middle of the night when everyone else was fast asleep. As he carried her along the glen, he wondered whether he really had been abandoned by the merfolk. Perhaps they had just moved south to warmer seas for the winter? Perhaps they would return in the spring and he'd find them there, feeding in his offshore waters? Perhaps they'd understand that he hadn't betrayed them after all?

He slipped into the freezing seas, and swam far out across the continental shelf to where the waters were deep and dark and still. Then he covered the little mermaid with stones, made the sign for sorrow and left her, in the ancient tradition of her own people, to feed the scuttling crabs.